3

MOTHER TWIN

Printed by Redwood Books, Kennet Way, Trowbridge

Published by Crossbridge Books
345 Old Birmingham Road
Bromsgrove, B60 1NX
Tel: 0121 447 7897

First published 2000

ISBN 0 9524604 7 5

British Library Cataloguing in Publication Data.
A catalogue record for this book is available from the
British Library.

Also by Eileen Mohr:

The Essential Book of Recipes for Good Living
The Kentle-Shaddy (novel for children aged 8-12)

MOTHER
TWIN

EILEEN MOHR

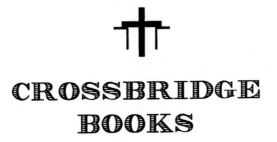

CROSSBRIDGE
BOOKS

Acknowledgement

The publisher wishes to express thanks to
E. M. Spencer for the words of the song,
"The Rose of Tralee".

1

As she stretched out a reluctant hand to switch off the alarm, Edith noticed the date that it displayed: Friday 13th March, 2020.

Friday the 13th! 'Don't start being superstitious now!' she told herself. 'You've got enough to contend with today, without thinking of extra bad luck.'

She knew that teaching would be a hard grind today, being conscious all the time that she would not be seeing Percelia after school, and then there was the meeting to follow. Ugh!

*   *   *   *   *   *   *

"Don't forget to record 'Jodie of the Jungle'," seven-year-old Celia shouted, as her friend Octavia ran to the front door of her home, which was next to Celia's.

"OK Perce," replied Octavia, "see you tomorrow!"

They had arrived home from school, and Mrs Green, who escorted the two girls to and from school along with her own eight-year-old daughter and five-year-old son, was curious.

"Why does Octavia call you 'Perce'?" she asked.

"Because my real name's Percelia. Grown-ups call me Celia, but the kids at school usually call me Perce or Percy."

"Oh, I see," responded Mrs Green. "Percelia is certainly a very unusual name, but it's quite pretty, like Priscilla. Bye-bye dear, see you on Monday."

"Bye."

It was a warm March, and there seemed to be more daffodils than ever in the front, unfenced gardens of the houses in this part of Cartford, Essex. Celia was usually inclined to take the glories of the natural world for granted, but today even she was struck by the beauty of the daffodils mingling with some blue grape hyacinths.

She rang the doorbell of her home, and was welcomed in with a warm hug by her adoptive mother.

"Auntie Edith will be here soon," she said, with a hint of warning in the tone. "I suppose you'll be able to do some homework after she's gone home."

"But don't forget it's Friday," Celia reminded her, "I can do it tomorrow, can't I?"

Her mother agreed that this was acceptable, so the girl ran upstairs to change out of her school uniform into a leisure suit.

"Can I have some apple juice, please?" she asked as soon as she was downstairs again.

"Well, I was going to suggest you wait till Auntie Edith has a cup of tea," Mrs Prentis replied, "but we don't know exactly what time she'll arrive, do we? So you may as well have it now," she said, smiling fondly as she went to the fridge.

There were two chocolate biscuits and one plain one on the plate, as Celia saw with delight, which she was given along with her plastic beaker of apple juice.

Her mother began to unplait her daughter's brown hair. "I'll just give your hair a quick comb through," she said, enjoying the sight of the reddish sheen which she thought rather beautiful as she combed. It was somehow irksome, however, that Auntie Edith had exactly the same colour hair as her daughter, as well as looking very much like her. 'I suppose her biological mother's hair was this colour', she thought, and was surprised at herself for the next thought that popped into her mind: 'But it would be surprising if her biological mother looked so much like her.'

Her own hair was dark blonde, which the sun lightened considerably when she gave it the opportunity. Her eyes were a pale blue, and although she was not pretty, she smiled so often and so warmly that people were generally inclined to describe her as "a lovely person".

June Prentis was easy-going and normally tolerant, but she found it hard to like Edith, who seemed to be unhealthily obsessed with monitoring her sister's child. It was like having an inspector calling every Friday to check that she was raising her adopted daughter correctly.

"Mum, Miss Armstrong said if we work in Mrs Thatcher's garden tomorrow, if it doesn't rain, she'll let us play Pirates in the gym on Monday instead of having PE."

"Oh, that'll be nice. The forecast is good for tomorrow, but they're expecting rain on Monday and Tuesday."

"I favour doing old people's gardens, and I *love* playing Pirates!"

The neighbourhood scheme that Celia was referring to involved the school, the local council and the Association of Local Churches, in which all collaborated to enable schoolchildren to acquire sufficient physical exercise to avert the danger of their becoming obese, which had become a problem around the turn of the century, whilst at the same time the children were helping the community.

Mrs Prentis put the comb away, fetched herself a cup of tea and came to join Celia in the living-room. She had just settled into an armchair to drink it, when the telephone rang, so she was about to get up again, but Celia beat her to it as she ran into the hallway to answer it.

Celia had guessed right. It was Auntie Edith.

"Hallo Celia. It's lovely to hear your voice. I'm sorry, it's impossible for me to come today, after all. We've got an emergency staff meeting that I have to attend. Would you ask your mummy if she would mind if I left it till next Friday, please?"

Mrs Prentis assured Auntie Edith that there was no problem, while Celia skipped and danced about the room with joy. She would be able to watch "Jodie of the Jungle" — one of her favourite TV programmes — after all!

Celia had mixed feelings about Auntie Edith's visits. They were always on a Friday, when it would have been nice to play with her friends after school, and they were almost as regular as clockwork, with the exception only of the school holidays, for she was a teacher, and usually went away for most of them.

Celia appreciated the chocolate bars which her aunt always brought for her on her visits, but there was something about Auntie Edith which made Celia feel uncomfortable. It was a bit creepy, and very often she was overcome with a certainty that her aunt was lying. It made her feel as bad as if she herself had just been discovered to have told a lie.

For Celia, this was serious. Her adoptive parents were keen Christians, and she had always enjoyed accompanying them to the Pentecostal church only two streets from where they lived. She herself had become a Christian about six months previously, when a man had come to the church to speak to the Sunday School children. He had explained how Jesus had suffered and died on the cross at Calvary to set us free from sin and hell. If anyone asked Him to be their Saviour, He would make it possible for them to live without committing sin.

Celia had known that this was exactly what she needed: she had usually tried to be good, but very often been unsuccessful. So she had responded to the man's offer to pray with any child at the end of Sunday School who wanted Jesus to save them. After the prayer, she had been filled with happiness. She knew that everything she had ever done or said that was wrong had been erased, and she could now always be obedient and truthful — wonderful!

And she had found, in the months following, that it was true! She was now obedient, kind and helpful, as she had promised in her prayer, and she would never tell a lie. And after her baptism by immersion she had felt even better — there was a wonderful freedom.

She switched on the television, and settled down happily to watch "Jodie of the Jungle", knowing that Octavia would have made a DVD of it on her machine, so they would be able to watch it again on the computer, either in Octavia's or her own bedroom.

Their respective parents allowed this, provided it ended no later than nine o'clock, and they had finished their homework.

The weather forecast had been right: it was a fine Saturday morning, and fifteen children had arrived at the school gates.

"That's good!" Miss Armstrong remarked, when she had counted them, "that's exactly half the class, so you'll be able to play Pirates on Monday instead of having PE."

When the cheering had finished, she divided them into three teams: one each to work on the gardens of elderly Mrs Thatcher, Mr Kinnock, and Mr Fowler, who lived next door to each other in a part of a neighbourhood containing fairly small, two-bedroomed houses.

Miss Armstrong checked with each of the residents that they still wanted the children's help. Mr Fowler and Mrs Thatcher welcomed the help, as they were both too incapacitated to do any gardening themselves, but Mr Kinnock thought he could work alongside the children.

"I've been having trouble getting about since I broke my hip," he said with a grimace, "but it's better than it was. I'll do a bit of pruning, while the youngsters do the weeding. OK?"

The teacher thought this would be acceptable, so she left him to supervise his team, while she did a round-up of each of the other gardens, reminding the children which were the weeds. Most of them remembered correctly from last year's frequent garden groundforces.

Celia and Octavia were in the team working on Mr Kinnock's garden. They were both good at recognising weeds, so they also kept an eye on what the other three were doing.

"Hey, Matthew," Octavia shouted suddenly, her dark brown hair bobbing about on her shoulders and her vivacious dark eyes sparkling with pride at her gardening expertise, "don't touch that! That's a pansy!"

"Thank you, dear," said Mr Kinnock with a benevolent smile, "it wouldn't have been too terrible if he'd pulled up a pansy, but I agree it would have been a pity."

When they had all finished, and were beaming at each other in satisfaction, Mr Kinnock brought out a bowl full of individually wrapped chocolates.

"There are thirty here," he announced, "I didn't know how many children would be coming."

"Fifteen!" one of the boys piped up. "That's two each!" he added.

"Oh-ho," said Mr Kinnock, smiling again, "so you're good at maths, as well as gardening!"

"Who would like to work on three other gardens next Saturday, weather permitting?" Miss Armstrong asked.

All the hands went up, amid shouts of "Me! Me!"

"Excellent! You'll be able to do Mrs Smith's, Mrs Brown's and Mrs Wilson's. And then there'll be Pirates again the following Monday!"

More cheering greeted this hoped-for announcement, as the children began to disperse.

As they walked home, munching their chocolates, Celia and Octavia agreed that they really favoured garden groundforces.

"But I'm looking forward to secondary school," Celia managed to say, in spite of the chocolate, "it'll be prima when we can help mums at home looking after their houses and small children!"

Her friend heartily agreed.

2

Edith realised, with a stab of annoyance as she caught
sight of her reflection in the mirror over the washbasin
in her neat, tastefully decorated bathroom, that the
irritation and frustration she had been feeling
throughout the meeting was still clearly visible on her
face.

She stared at the reflection for a few more
moments, consciously attempting to compose her
features into a more serene expression, and being
reminded, as ever, that her chin was just a little bit too
long for her face to be considered attractive. Her
nose, she thought, wasn't bad — perhaps slightly too big
for most people's taste, at least in Britain, but she knew
that most people in the Middle East would consider it
normal. Her hair was medium brown, with quite an
attractive reddish sheen when freshly washed. As for
her eyes, blue-grey with fairly long, dark lashes, they
ought to be her best feature. Yet as she looked into
them, something seemed to be not quite right . . . it
was probably because of the child, she concluded. But

the compulsion to keep on seeing her, to watch her progress, was irresistible.

She looked at her watch. 10.30. It had been a long meeting, and as deputy head of her comprehensive school it had taken a tremendous amount of nervous energy to keep most of the other members of staff on her side against the headteacher.

To her, there was really not a problem. The Muslim girls attending the school wanted, or of course in most cases their parents, wanted them to wear their traditional headscarves covering their hair while in school. Edith considered it ludicrous for the headteacher, Ken Hacksby, to try to insist on banning the headscarves. It was obvious to Edith that the ethical solution was to allow them, since the girls — or their parents — believed it to be the right thing to do.

She felt too tired to do even a minimal amount of cooking. A piece of fruit cake and a cup of decaf would have to do, and then bed.

Sleep, however, eluded her for most of the night. She missed seeing Celia. Was she getting the best kind of upbringing? Was she getting enough love from her adoptive parents? Was she at the right kind of school? Would she be able to go to the right kind of secondary school?

Some of the schools in Cartford had been well below standard a decade or two earlier. There had been continual problems with truancy and loutish behaviour, as well as abysmally low grades. But they had improved considerably recently, so perhaps one of them would be good enough by the time Celia reached secondary age.

Would she go on to further education? David Prentis was a pleasant enough person, but was he a sufficiently good father to provide for all that Celia was going to need?

The Government was in the process of phasing out student loans, and were repeatedly briefing the media with promises of grants for the tuition fees of all students who were accepted by universities, plus accommodation grants according to parental income. It sounded quite hopeful . . .

Her thoughts wandered among the possible universities where she might study for a degree: Oxford? Probably not. Cambridge . . .? 'I don't suppose Jonathan is still there . . He may have a professorship by now . . . He wouldn't if it became public knowledge what happened seven years ago . . . well, it isn't going to . . . She might want to go to one of the other universities in some of the more beautiful parts of the country . . . Exeter, Wales, . . .one of the Scottish ones . . . St Andrew's . . .

'I suppose she'll do languages. That'll be useful — we can practise our languages on each other . . . but she may want to do Spanish or Russian. That would be good motivation to learn them . . . comprendo perfectamente bien . . . . do svidanya.

'What if she wants to get married young and not go to university? I would hate that. It would be a waste of her brains . . . But if she made up her mind, there wouldn't be much use trying to stop her. She probably wouldn't listen to me anyway . . .'

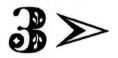

3

Although Celia loved her adoptive mother dearly, she also loved her real maternal grandmother, whom she called "Grandma", just about as much. June's mother, Grannie, lived in Carlisle with Grandpops, and Grannie Prentis in Ballater, Scotland, so Celia didn't see them very often. Her biological father's parents were in Australia, and never wrote to her or telephoned; but she hoped to meet them one day.

When Celia was old enough to be told that her real mother and father had died in a fire in Australia when she was a baby, Grandma had comforted her in such a sweet, tender way that Celia had been able to accept the tragic story without too much pain. Yet she longed to know more about the mother who had given birth to her.

"Can't you find any more photos of her, Grandma?" she asked, for what seemed the zillionth time, as she sat at the big table in Grandma's pleasantly furnished, comfortable sitting room in Rayleigh, Essex, looking at photographs and albums. She was now nine years old, and had so far seen only very few.

"Well, I should have a lot more, somewhere, but I still haven't managed to find the others yet. It's all Grandad's fault," Grandma said with an impish grin which made her face, which was pleasantly attractive, look much more so.

Her eyes were blue-grey like Celia's and Auntie Edith's, her straight nose neither too big nor too small, and her hair, although now showing grey or silver curls, still had some dark brown areas. "He had too many different jobs, which involved moving around too much," she explained.

Celia knew that her grandmother was not being unkind in saying this, even though her grandfather had died three years before; she knew that he would simply have joined in the little joke.

"Well, I'm certainly very much like my real mum," she observed. "And if you keep looking, maybe you'll find some photos of Mum Number One with you and Grandad and Auntie Edith."

"Yes, they must be around somewhere," Grandma agreed. "I'll go and put the kettle on."

She went to the side door of her large, well-equipped kitchen and called to David and June Prentis, who had been admiring the garden in the meantime.

"Your garden's looking better than I've ever seen it!" David enthused as they came back into the house.

"Well, it is July, and I do have a gardener who comes for a couple of hours twice a week," said Grandma modestly. "But I agree it's looking lovely at the moment."

June helped Grandma make sandwiches while David and Celia had another look at the photos. There were some of Auntie Edith aged about five in the garden of the house where they were living at the time. Some of Celia's biological mother aged seven and nine at the seaside, some when she was about eleven, in a different garden.

They heard a car pull onto the drive at the front of the house, and saw that, behind David and June's car, it was Auntie Edith who was emerging from the Jaguar which had just arrived.

She seemed somewhat agitated to see Celia's parents.

"Oh, hallo there. I just popped over to bring this video . . . Hallo Mum, I can only stop for a little while

— I'm up to my ears in reports needing to be done . . . "

Edith was persuaded to stay to tea, at least, and she was invited by Celia to have another look at the old photographs

"Look," the girl said in a challenging tone, "Grandma can only find these few photos of your sister, but quite a lot of you. Surely you've got some, haven't you? There must be some of the two of you when you were playing together!"

Edith looked at the photos, and commented, "You're probably right. I must have some of Margaret somewhere."

Celia suddenly knew that Auntie Edith was lying. It was as clear to her and as painful as if she herself had just been caught lying. She stared at her aunt, who had not been looking in her direction as she spoke, but now looked at her — and turned pale. Edith was horrified by what she could read in the girl's eyes.

She went into the kitchen. "I'm sorry Mum, I'll have to go after all. I've got a headache now. I must get back and take something for it. Maybe if I lie down for a bit I'll be able to get on with the reports."

She was allowed to depart amid commiserating farewells, and Celia was left wondering what to make of her aunt's bizarre behaviour.

Grandma's delicious hazelnut cake took her mind off the subject, as she and her parents gave expression to their appreciation.

"I wish I could manage to produce such a good cake," said June. "I've tried to make one, following your recipe, but each time it turned out a soggy mess!"

"You have to make sure the egg white is *really* stiff, and that involves taking the eggs out of the fridge a good while before you start, so they're at room temperature, and make sure you don't use any egg white that's still liquid at the bottom of the basin," Grandma advised.

June promised to have another try, which elicited hopeful murmurs from her husband and daughter.

"I'm sure we'd all appreciate that!" said David.

"It would be absomagnous if it worked!" declared Celia.

They all enjoyed a game of Scrabble, won, as usual, by Grandma. Then it was time to go, and Celia and her parents arrived home at the nine-year-old's bedtime.

June was in the process of settling her daughter in bed for the night, when her beloved child began what at first sounded like a delaying tactic.

"Mum," Celia said in that familiar tone signalling a tricky question or possibly heart-rending confession to follow, "why does Auntie Edith behave in such a strange way sometimes?"

The question was a difficult one to answer.

"How d'you mean — 'strange'?"

"Well, like the way she suddenly went white when I asked her about photos of her with her sister, and then suddenly having to go home."

"I don't know, really," her mother answered slowly, "maybe she's finding it hard to cope with being deputy head of her school. Anyway, if it worries you, the best thing to do is to pray for Auntie Edith. Ask God to help her and take care of her."

"But she doesn't go to church — I'm not sure whether she's a Christian," Celia protested.

"You can still pray for her, whether she's a Christian or not. God will grant your prayers because it's you — His daughter — who's asking Him."

"Oh, all right, that's what I'll do then," Celia replied with satisfaction in her tone. "Night-night Mum."

June gave her a goodnight kiss. "Night-night dear. God bless you."

"Thank you. God bless you, too."

CHAPTER THREE

As her mother put out the light and closed the bedroom door, Celia began her prayers contentedly, including some for Auntie Edith. It was incredibly easy to visualise her, as she liked to do for each person being prayed for, because she only needed to visualise her own face in the mirror, but just with the brown hair cut short and combed over to the left.

4

Edith tried for the umpteenth time to start the engine of her Jaguar. There was no response.

'Oh well,' she thought, 'at least it's not a school day. I'll just have to ring the AA for Home Start.'

It was now 2023, and the end of the late May half-term holidays. She had arrived back from Italy the day before, after an enjoyable week in Florence with her friend, Janice.

Edith had got into her car late in the morning after sleeping in until 9.30, intending to visit her mother.

The AA man arrived after about a quarter of an hour, and investigated why the car wouldn't start. He had soon got it started, and reversed a few feet along the drive. The car continued on its backward course, however, when he attempted to brake . . . He hastily grabbed the handbrake, and the car came to a stop.

"Whew!" he shouted to Edith, who was still standing near the house, wondering what was going on. "Lucky your drive's long enough for this game!"

He bent down to look at the brake, then got out and looked around for some large stones or bricks. Edith found him some stones that were big enough to prevent the car from rolling, and he disappeared underneath the vehicle.

After a few minutes he reappeared, looking at Edith with concern.

"You must have a guardian angel!" he declared in a shocked voice. "You were lucky it wouldn't start. The brakes have been cut!"

Edith couldn't believe her ears. "Cut?" she echoed incredulously. "Are you sure?"

"I'm afraid so," he replied. "No doubt about it."

The police came and took the car away for forensic examination, and Edith was interviewed at the police station.

"Is there anyone who could be described as your 'enemy'?" she was asked.

"No," she replied with a hint of a laugh, "I don't have any enemies!"

"Can you think of anyone who harbours a grudge against you?"

"No, I can't think of anyone," she answered. She was a strict disciplinarian at school, but always fair, and she knew, from what colleagues had told her, that the students respected her for this.

25

"I'm sure it wasn't any of the students," she declared, "and I can't imagine any of the staff doing a thing like this."

Leaving the police to continue their enquiries, Edith hired a small two-door car to keep mobile in the meantime.

Her mother found it equally difficult to believe that someone had tried to kill her daughter. But she agreed that she must have a guardian angel.

"So the AA man seemed to be saying that if the car had started normally this morning, you would probably have been killed!"

"Apparently," Edith agreed.

"Someone must have been praying for you," her mother concluded. "I pray a bit, but not as regularly as I'm sure a lot of other people do, including June and David."

"Mm-m, maybe it was one of them," said her daughter thoughtfully. Edith considered herself to be a Christian, as she had begun to tell everyone so in 2008, when the Great Revival was at its height. But her belief was only superficial; she had never made a commitment to Jesus Christ.

The weather was so beautiful that they decided to take their minds off the inexplicable incident by enjoying their tea on the patio in the garden at the rear of the house. However, the old problem of Celia's ongoing quest for photographs surfaced afresh in Edith's mind.

"How can we manage to get two shots of me on one photograph?" Edith asked her mother querulously, as she sipped her tea. The Friday visits would soon be resuming. "I don't suppose Boots or any of the others who do photography would do it."

"I know someone who does photography at home," her mother announced. "He sells birthday cards at the market. He probably wouldn't mind doing it."

"OK, ask him to put this photo of me about fifteen with this one of me aged about eleven," Edith said, as she extracted them from her shoulder bag.

Her mother studied the two photographs. The background of each showed a garden. There didn't seem to be any tell-tale landmarks which would give anything away.

"Yes, I'll tell him I'd like an enlargement to put in a frame. That will be quite true."

"Oh good," Edith breathed, "maybe that will stop Celia pestering us for a while."

Feeling somewhat reassured, she sank back into the garden chair and exhaled slowly. As she then drew a deep breath, she became aware of the superbly sweet fragrance of the shrubs a few feet away. She had been too preoccupied until then to notice them or the other flowers and bushes in her mother's garden. It sloped down more than a hundred metres — mainly well-kept lawn, but with decorative steps on the left-hand side in front of beds of anemones, behind which grew multi-coloured flowers whose name she didn't know, and behind them were early lupins and hollyhocks interspersed with delphiniums. On the right-hand side there was a wide path flanked by a variety of shrubs and mini-conifers, leading down to a stream at the bottom of the garden.

Beyond Mother's garden a panorama of trees which grew in the neighbours' large gardens could be seen. The various green tints of the foliage produced a superb colour composition: mid-green oaks, dark green cypresses, lighter green ash, pale green willow and the delicate tracery of birch.

"I see you're appreciating the view for a change," Edith's mother commented. "I'm very fortunate to live here. Apart from the fact that all the inundations of the sea and the Thames that have covered most of the lower parts of Rayleigh left us high and dry, I love the trees.

"Remember when Dad worked in the Middle East? It was just wonderful to see the trees again when we came home. After that, I'll never stop admiring the beauty of trees. I really love them!"

"I wasn't out there long enough to miss them as you did," Edith remarked.

* * * * * * *

On the next Friday visit Edith took some old photographs which she had found, plus the montage showing herself at different ages in the same garden scene. An old briefcase from her student days was useful to carry them in.

Celia, now aged ten, had walked home from school this Friday with Octavia and Mrs Green's daughter Rebecca, whose younger brother Robin was ill. June Prentis and Octavia's mother had assured Mrs Green on the telephone that they thought it would be all right for the girls to come home without her company.

Since the Great Revival which had swept through the United Kingdom in 2008, when people began flocking into the churches in repentance, seeking God's forgiveness, so that by the end of 2009 approximately 85% of the population were committed Christians, crime had fallen dramatically. Hardly any of the muggings, burglaries, rapes, or murders which had been so common, were ever known to be committed, and there was very little drug-taking or drunkenness.

Consequently it was really quite safe to allow children to move about outside on their own. It was simply that the tradition of escorting them to and from school towards the end of the last century had become so entrenched that it was difficult to break out of the pattern.

Celia waited with resignation for Auntie Edith's visit. But this changed to excitement when she heard her aunt announce that she had found some more photos at last! Auntie Edith sat down on the sofa next to her, took a few out of the briefcase and handed them to the eager girl.

"Is this you — or Mum Number 1?" she asked dubiously.

Auntie Edith leaned forward to get a closer view. "This is me . . . so is this . . ." then she took out the composite photograph. "I found this one of the two of us!" she declared triumphantly.

Celia studied the photograph delightedly, but as she glanced up at her aunt, there again was that certainty that she was lying! She flung the photograph onto the sofa and ran upstairs.

June, who was in the kitchen preparing the evening meal, was unaware of what had happened, so she was taken aback to be confronted by Edith, obviously upset, telling her that she needed to go home; she had forgotten some important school work that she must do.

"Oh, I'm cooking German sausages — Bratwurst — one of your favourites. Are you sure you can't stay?"

For a nanosecond Edith seemed to hesitate, but then repeated that she had to go.

June closed the front door after waving her goodbye, and looked thoughtfully to see what Celia was doing. Not there. Where was she?

"Are you upstairs, Celia?" she called.

There was a muffled reply, giving June greater concern. She hurried upstairs to find her daughter lying on her bed, sobbing.

"Whatever's the matter dear?" June asked gently.

"Auntie Edith . . . upset . . . me!" came the answer between sobs.

June put her arm around her daughter, asking, "How did she do that?"

There was no reply; only renewed sobbing.

"Can't you tell me what upset you — please?"

"No-(sob)-o-(sob)-o!"

June concluded that it was no use trying to force Celia to confide in her. She would just have to leave her to recover from the upset in her own way.

She descended the stairs, wondering what David would think. He was normally jovial and friendly with everyone, but if something or someone provoked him in what he considered an injustice, he could sometimes erupt in fury.

When David heard about the incident, as June was serving up the food in the kitchen and Celia was still upstairs, he was silent for a few moments. Then he said, "I think we'd better pray about it when Celia's gone to bed, OK?"

His wife agreed that this would be a good idea, so no more was said about it. Their daughter came downstairs with red, puffy eyes, but managed to enjoy the Bratwurst. David even soon succeeded in getting her to laugh.

"Speaking of sausage reminds me of something my Uncle Jack once told me," he said. "In the days when the telephonists had a bit more talking to do in the office where he worked, one of them said on the phone to a Mr Liversedge, 'Good morning Mr Liversausage'!"

Once Celia had been tucked up in bed and kissed goodnight, David and June spent a few minutes praying about the situation. A few more minutes of silence, then David said:

"I think we should leave it till tomorrow, and then decide how to handle it."

"That sounds like good sense," his wife responded. She knew how much better this policy was than reacting immediately in a rage.

Next morning, before leaving to go to his work in an accountants' office, David told June that he had come to the conclusion that they should not be too hard on Edith this time, but if anything similar should happen again, she should be asked to stay away from Celia.

June expressed her willingness to go along with this proposal, so there the matter rested.

5

In spite of there having been no more discernible attempts on her life, Edith had a sense of foreboding. She had taken a number of precautions, as advised by the police, including using only hired cars; staying sometimes at her friend Janice's flat in Brentwood; sometimes with her mother and sometimes at hotels.

Staying in her job would obviously be risky, she thought. She would have to confide in the head-teacher, Mr Hacksby, who was in his fifties, and a generally pleasant, helpful person, though sometimes inclined to be over-conscientious.

"I agree," he said gravely, when Edith explained the situation. "We'll sorely miss you, but I think I can probably arrange for you to be fast-tracked as an English Assistant in France or Germany for a year. Would that meet with your approval?"

"It certainly would, if you can arrange it. Thanks very much."

There were no places available in a French school, but Edith was told she could start her year as an English Assistant at a Gymnasium in Mannheim, Germany.

She told the rest of the staff that she was going away for a year "on a secret assignment", which she wanted to be kept confidential. There were some raised eyebrows at this, but most thought it was a bit of a joke.

On the last day of term Mr Hacksby persuaded Edith to let him tell the rest of the staff at a special, brief meeting, that an attempt had been made on her life. He was sure, he said, that they would keep the matter confidential, so that *anyone* asking about her whereabouts should be told simply that Edith was no longer at the school.

Her mother offered to spend half of each week in Edith's house, so as to keep it in good order.

"Oh, that's really prima!" exclaimed Edith. "I was considering renting it out, but of course that could be problematic. I do have enough savings to keep the standing order for the mortgage going. Thank you very much, Mum!"

The Direktor of the Karl-Friedrich Gymnasium wrote to Edith, giving her three names and addresses of possible lodgings where she could stay in Mannheim.

The first one, with a Frau Behagel, sounded acceptable and inexpensive. Edith would be living on a small grant, and as she had not been in the habit of saving much, except in earlier years for the deposit on her house, then for the Jaguar, most of her saving these days was for her holidays. So she decided to try to live on the grant.

The Mannheim dialect was incredibly different from any other she had heard hitherto, and compared unfavourably with all the others, she thought: Austrian, Swiss German, the Low German spoken in northern areas such as Hamburg — those sounded attractive to her ears, but the Mannheim version was really unpleasant, in Edith's opinion.

She had a bedsitter in the Behagel family's flat, which was not very large, but she supposed she could survive for a year. Herr and Frau Behagel were a young couple in their twenties, with a little daughter Ingrid, aged six, who was soon calling the new lady in their home "die engelische Tante".

Edith chuckled to herself at the thought of being described as "the angelic aunt".

The worst part of Edith's new life was the morning

scramble into the Strassenbahn, to arrive at school by 8 o'clock. The Revival had only been spreading its effect in Germany for about four years, and consequently there was still a great deal of avoidable pushing and elbowing at each stop, from Zeppelinstrasse to her stop near the Wasserturm.

The Strassenbahn itself was a credit to its designers: smooth running, quiet and with comfortable seats, so that it was a pleasure to travel on one at non-peak times. Edith wondered why they seemed to be more comfortable than the latest British trams, but without engineering knowledge, she was unable to explain it.

The Gymnasium was an impressive, stately building, but lacking any adjacent playing fields. To play football or other sports the students were obliged to travel some distance from the school. For break times there was simply an asphalted area.

The reversed role of teaching English to German students appealed greatly to Edith. It was most enjoyable — until she was asked to give some extra conversation lessons to below-grade students at **7.30** on several mornings! As she mentioned in a letter to her mother, she complied with the request, but it was always a struggle to get up at that antisocial hour.

Edith used a post box in Rayleigh for her letters to her mother, and the latter omitted her own address in her answering letters, as a further precaution. They had agreed that it wouldn't be wise to telephone each other.

The worst thing about being so far away from Cartford was, of course, not being able to see Celia. Not even to be able to write to her, for that could give away her location. Not to know how she was progressing was misery, so that what would otherwise have been a most enjoyable year was always edged with unhappiness.

Nevertheless, there were compensations. One was her friendship with Frau Buhler, the senior English teacher. Monika Buhler, like herself, was unmarried, and was delighted to have the companionship of this woman who spoke perfect English.

At first, during the English lessons Frau Buhler seated Edith at the back of the class to listen to the lesson as it proceeded, and occasionally called on her to read a passage of English. The teacher's enthusiastic reception of Edith's reading was so heartfelt that the Englishwoman was both embarrassed and amused by its intensity.

"That was a wonderful reading!" she exclaimed after the first of these, when Edith read from T.S. Eliot's *The Cocktail Party*. "I have never heard such beautiful English!"

Their patronage of a café near the water tower, a landmark which had been restored after the Second World War to its former ornate splendour, for afternoon coffee and cake became so habitual that, when Monika realised that Edith was on a tight budget, she insisted on paying the bill, every time.

"I favour your company," she declared. "I favour talking to you, whether in English or in German."

When the Christmas season was approaching, Edith discovered another compensation. The weeks of Advent were given a magical quality through a tradition observed by a great many people. Monika, who repeatedly made Edith feel at home in her comfortable yet elegant flat, made her feel welcome each time, but particularly during advent. She had made an advent wreath, containing four red candles, one to be lit for each Sunday leading up to Christmas. It was suspended from a hook in the ceiling, and on the coffee table and on the sideboard were further decorative arrangements consisting of candles, fir twigs and cones.

Edith had to agree with her German friend that she, too, favoured talking to her, no matter whether in German or English, and the candlelight made the room really gemütlich.

Christmas itself was even more magical, and more meaningful than in most households in Britain, Edith thought. The important day was Christmas Eve, which Edith spent with the Behagel family.

Ingrid had to stay in the kitchen throughout the afternoon, helping her mother make special Christmas biscuits, some consisting mainly of almonds, others of spicy Lebkuchen, while some were of a plainer texture, but cut into a wide variety of different shapes: animals, stars, or geometrical patterns. There had been no sign of a Christmas tree.

Then, about six o'clock, everyone, including Ingrid's paternal grandparents, who had arrived about half an hour earlier, was allowed into the living-room. The only lighting came from the candles on the Christmas tree, which had suddenly and mysteriously appeared in the corner of the room, and from other candles placed judiciously around the room.

Herr Behagel picked up his guitar, and everyone joined in singing some of the best-known carols, including, of course, "Silent Night".

Only after about five carols had been sung did Herr Behagel take the presents one by one from under the Christmas tree and distribute them to the rest of the family. Needless to say, Ingrid's delight at her presents was shared by everyone else: a doll's pram from her parents, a most beautiful teddy bear from her grandparents, and a wonderful doll from Edith.

The "engelische Tante" herself received a very pleasant surprise in the form of a wooden-backed hand-mirror which had been beautifully carved by Ingrid's grandfather into a rose.

"Opa", as Ingrid called him, was a frequent visitor to the Behagels' flat, so Edith knew him well; but she had been unaware of his skill in wood-carving.

"Thank you so much. It's really beautiful," she told him, feeling that her expression of thanks was inadequate. "I didn't know you were such a skilful craftsman."

"I enjoy carving," he replied with a gentle smile.

After she had been in Mannheim for approximately five months, during which she had gradually come to accept the local dialect as spoken by some of her less affluent friends, who seemed to make it a constant vehicle for never-ending humour, so that it became a pleasantly familiar sound, she was introduced to some new friends at the church that she had been attending.

They had been chatting after the service for about ten minutes, when Helga, one of the new friends, suddenly exclaimed:

"Ach! You are English! I thought you were German!"

A glow of deep satisfaction spread through Edith's body as she heard the words. It was a goal she had been aiming at for several years, and at last she had reached it.

Her joy turned suddenly to anxiety, however, when she noticed that the man who appeared to be Helga's friend, and who came from Columbia, was looking at her with what seemed to be acute interest.

A chill settled over her, listening to the Latin American accent which pervaded his German conversation, as he probed into her background, and his eyes examined her with a strange intensity.

Her attempt to avoid further exchange of pleasantries with these new acquaintances was successful. She was able to casually join another group, and after a few minutes wished them a pleasant Sunday, whereupon she had no difficulty making her way out of the building.

The nagging question remained in her head, however: could this man be looking for her, and if so, why?

6

Throughout the time in Germany and since then Edith had not been aware of anything that could realistically be considered sinister. Her anxiety about the man from Latin America had apparently been groundless, for there had been no attempt to harm her, as far as she knew. She was now hopeful that whoever it was had given up the idea of trying to kill her.

It was the beginning of the summer holidays in 2027, and she had agreed to postpone her customary trip to the Continent or Eastern Europe so that Celia could stay with her for a few days. David Prentis was due to attend a course in Wales in connection with his work, and he wanted June to take the opportunity to spend some time there with him, enjoying the Welsh mountains.

There was no apparent reason why Celia should not spend a few days at her home, Edith thought to herself. While she had been in Germany her mother had arranged for her house to be sold, and Edith was quite happy with the new one her mother had bought on her behalf. It was a two-bedroomed, semi-detached house on the edge of Bishops Stortford instead of near the centre; close enough for convenient car travel to her school in Cartford, yet far enough away for her to be only rarely seen by any of the students outside of school hours.

David and June brought Celia on Sunday afternoon after lunch, as they wanted to arrive at their destination in Wales that evening, thus enabling David to attend the first sessions on Monday morning.

Celia was now fourteen, and looking even more like Edith than ever. When her parents had set off again on their way, Edith gave Celia one of her strange looks, and commented, "Goodness, you're nearly as tall as me now!"

"I could probably wear some of your clothes, too!" Celia responded hopefully.

Edith had arranged a trip to a safari park, using an old Land-Rover which she had borrowed from one of the chemistry teachers, who said he didn't mind if the monkeys scratched it. It was so old that it stemmed from the time when they were made of aluminium, which doesn't rust, and scratches could be simply painted over.

"That was very kind of him!" exclaimed Celia, when her aunt gave her this piece of information. She was always fascinated by monkeys, so she could hardly wait until they reached that area.

It immediately seemed that the Land-Rover was being taken over by the appealing, inquisitive little creatures trying to get in through the closed windows, touching, pulling and tweaking everything possible to touch, pull or tweak.

It was the highlight of the trip for Celia, particularly the tiny monkeys, which looked only a week or two old.

"I wish we could open the window!" Celia exclaimed longingly.

"No chance," replied her aunt. "We'd never get rid of them, apart from the fact that it's against the rules."

Celia had not mentioned to Auntie Edith the feeling of panic she always experienced when first getting into a car. It had been going on for several years now, but she knew that all she had to do was pray, and the feeling would leave her.

They enjoyed observing the rest of the animals, especially the lions and tigers, which didn't look at all predatory in their well-fed state of health, then they stopped off for a bite to eat.

This time, after they had got back into the car, and Celia had dealt with her problem by prayer, she told her aunt about the panicky feeling.

Auntie Edith reacted in a very odd way. She looked at her niece, and was just beginning to say, "Oh, so — ," when she seemed to choke, and began a fit of coughing which Celia knew to be false. She then said, "Well, I'm glad the attacks don't last long."

Celia thought, 'Here we go again . . .', but decided to try to forget that her aunt was lying once more.

Next morning, after breakfast Auntie Edith told Celia, to her delight, that she could try on some of her clothes if she liked.

"There are some dresses in that little wardrobe in your room," she said. "And I think there are some tops in some of the drawers that might look quite good on you."

It was a suggestion that greatly appealed to the girl, so she amused herself for about an hour trying on various dresses. They both agreed that some of them really suited her.

Then came the tops. She found several cotton ones, two velour, and a few silky ones. Underneath these, there were some pieces of paper and a photograph.

It showed a girl of her own age in school uniform. Celia stared at it. The uniform was not that of her school, yet she seemed to be looking at a photograph of herself!

She had picked up some of the pieces of paper along with the photograph, and her glance was caught by some letters, apparently written by someone trying out an anagram:

REPLICAE
PERCELIA

Indescribable feelings of curiosity, frustration and impotence struggled for supremacy within her. She marched down into the small dining-room where Edith had installed her compunicunit, box files and books as a study area at one end, and was now engaged in sorting her computer files into better order.

Celia cleared her throat to alert her aunt to her presence, then, in a voice she was striving to control, she asked, "And who might this be then?"

"Computer, save file and close," said Edith quickly, as the screen was querying Celia's question. Although the latter's intonation tended to be different from her aunt's, the machine had reacted to what it interpreted as the same vocal patterns.

As on previous occasions, when she looked at the photograph the colour left Auntie Edith's face. She blinked rapidly, saying, "Er, that's your Mum number 1 when she was your age."

Celia knew that this was untrue.

"And what about this?" she demanded, holding the piece of paper with the anagram under her aunt's nose. "Am I just imagining that this word was meant to be 'Percelia'?"

"Let me see," Edith murmured, taking the piece of paper. Then she glanced up at Celia. "You're very inquisitive, aren't you? It's obviously something someone was playing around with to make an anagram, isn't it."

"That looks to me as if it was 'Percelia'," her niece persisted in a challenging tone.

"And all the person could come up with was 'replica', with an 'e' left over!" said Auntie Edith with a hint of triumph, screwing up the paper into a ball and tossing it into the waste-paper basket.

But Celia knew, as before, that her aunt was hiding the truth. This time she was in no mood to keep quiet about it.

"You're lying!" she shouted furiously. "What's it all about? Why do you keep lying to me?"

"Don't be silly, dear," her aunt said, attempting a soothing voice, "of course I'm not lying!"

"Oh yes you are! And even if you won't tell me the truth now, one day I'll find out!" Celia's words flooded out in a torrent, then she ran upstairs and began packing her belongings.

When Edith mounted the stairs to see what her niece was doing, Celia turned to face her and said, with an air of authority which could have matched any of this deputy head's:

"I want you to take me to Octavia's. I'm not staying here one moment longer than I can help. And it would probably be an advantage if I could phone them first!"

Edith realised that it would be pointless to try to keep the girl here, so she allowed her to telephone her best friend.

Octavia's mother, Charlotte Masson, who did some editorial and proofreading work at home, had no objection to letting Celia stay there until her parents returned from Wales.

7

Having dropped Celia off at Octavia's house in Cartford, Edith knew, as she drove back to Bishops Stortford, what people meant when they claimed to feel "shattered". The word really did describe exactly how she felt.

The worst thing was that Celia's parents were sure to forbid her to have any contact with her niece in future. The prospect was unbearable. And the thought that Celia now seemed to hate her was almost as painful.

She mooched about the house, from one room to another, as if in a trance. She folded the clothes Celia had been trying on, and put them away. Then she flopped into an armchair in the lounge and stared at nothing.

The day dragged on until her fears were realised. The telephone rang that evening at about half past nine. It was June, wanting to ask Celia whether she had enjoyed her day.

Edith had no option but to tell her what had happened. "I didn't mean to upset her," she added, but sounded rather unconvincing, even to herself.

There was silence at the other end of the line for a few moments, then June replied, "Stay there a moment, please. I'll just get David."

As Edith had anticipated, he was angry. "What d'you mean by upsetting her again!" came loudly and full of fury down the line. "We're not going to put up with it any longer! You've done it before, but this is the last time! We don't want you visiting us ever again in future. D'you understand?"

"I really am sorry," Edith said, struggling to control the tears which were forcing their way into her eyes and affecting her voice, "but I understand what you're saying. I hope I'll be allowed to see her again some day."

"I don't know about that. We'll have to wait and see," said David, less angrily. "Goodbye."

Edith reached for the tissues on the sideboard and sank into an armchair, sobbing. 'If only I had put the photo somewhere she would never have found it! . . . And the anagram . . . how could I have left it in one of those drawers?!' She then remembered that the removal men had said it didn't matter if she left things in the drawers: they would be all right during the move. 'How am I going to survive without seeing Celia?' she wondered.

Octavia was delighted that Celia would be staying with her family for a few days, although she was disappointed that her best friend wouldn't confide in her about what had upset her at Auntie Edith's. Celia told her simply that she would rather not talk about it.

Her mother didn't have any urgent work to finish, so after lunch, when they had all contributed to washing and drying the dishes, Charlotte thought it might help if Celia were encouraged to talk. But Celia's thoughts were no longer centred on Auntie Edith.

Her History teacher had been dealing with the Methodist Revival of the eighteenth century, explaining how it brought about enormous changes for the better in British society. She knew that Octavia's mother had a good memory for facts and figures, and she wanted to hear more about life before the Great Revival.

They sat in the comfortable, floral-covered armchairs at one end of the lounge, and Charlotte, ignoring the typescripts waiting to be edited on the table at the other end, dredged up memories of pre-2008 years.

"Well, you know all about the murders, muggings and rapes that used to go on, so that almost all women and girls were afraid to go out at night on their own," she began; "did you know that the hospitals used to be overcrowded, so that patients — even elderly ones — were often left lying for hours on trolleys in the corridors?"

"No, I didn't know about that," replied Celia, shocked and horrified.

"Neither did I," added Octavia. "That was horrorful!"

"Didn't the churches offer Divine healing?" Celia asked in surprise.

"Only relatively few. And don't forget that only a small percentage of the population went to any kind of church regularly. Most of the people ignored the Church, except perhaps for some weddings and funerals, and they just refused to believe any stories about Divine healing.

"But, of course," Charlotte continued, "there wouldn't have been anything like as much sickness if people hadn't taken so many drugs or drunk so much alcohol, or smoked so much, and if they hadn't always been so worried about everything. All those things made people ill, and especially the worry. That used to cause all kinds of problems, including stomach ulcers or duodenal ulcers, or gallstones, or heart attacks."

"What about the schools?" Octavia enquired. "What were they like?"

"Some were not too bad, but a lot of them had problems with students — mostly boys — who had no intention of learning anything, and simply spent their time disrupting the lessons until they were ordered to stay away."

"Told to stay away!" Celia repeated incredulously. "How crazy! So what did these boys do then?"

"They often took drugs, and stole or broke into houses to get the money to keep their habit going," Charlotte explained sadly, "and then of course they usually finished up as criminals."

"It's hard to believe people were so stupid!" Celia commented.

"Well, when people ignore God and His laws, that He gave us for our benefit, that's the kind of thing that's sure to happen," said Charlotte. "They thought they were so clever, they didn't need God!"

When it was time for a cup of tea, Charlotte produced a chocolate bar for each to enjoy, at which point Celia remarked:

"I may not miss Auntie Edith, but I'll miss her choccy bars, Occy!"

During the following three days Charlotte found

herself telling the two girls a great deal more about life before 2008. Her husband, Peter, also shared his memories.

"I remember what a problem clothes were, when I was at school. Pretty well all the children wore something called 'trainers' on their feet, and they had to be a particular brand, which were extremely expensive. My parents didn't want to waste their money on them, but they didn't want me to have to put up with being laughed at, or even bullied, if I didn't have them."

"Oorgh, I'm glad I didn't live around the turn of the century!" said Octavia.

"So am I! It's hard to understand how stupid people could be," Celia commented.

"Did you hate being alive?" Octavia asked.

"No, I didn't," her mother replied, "but a lot of teenagers did. There were far too many suicides among young people. Or a lot of the girls almost died through anorexia."

"What was that?" queried Celia.

"They used to be influenced by very thin models in magazines and in adverts on television, so they ate less and less, to try to get slim, until they became really ill. And I'm afraid the fat girls quite often got bullied."

"At the end of the last century it could be pretty

awful to be old, as well," said Peter. "Senior citizens got only a very small state pension — only about twenty percent of the average wage, even though they'd worked hard all their lives. In the 1980s a lot of them died from hypothermia — simply being too cold, because they couldn't afford to pay to keep themselves warm!"

"And they only sometimes got help with keeping their houses and gardens neat and tidy," Charlotte added. "If they wanted someone to clean their house, they usually had to pay towards it, and a lot of them couldn't afford that. As for their gardens, they were lucky if some volunteers from a church youth group helped them occasionally. They didn't have the neighbourhood schemes with the schools that we have now."

"What else was awful before 2008?" asked Octavia.

"Quite a lot, including the high divorce rate, so that in some schools half the children were from one-parent families!"

"Whew!" came from both girls together.

"Didn't they have parenting classes?" Celia queried.

"No, very few schools had them. They had their priorities wrong," said Charlotte. "And a lot of the broken marriages were probably caused partly by the promiscuity among young people. Only a very small percentage kept their virginity until they were married. So the physical bond was cheapened, and again, they had the wrong priorities."

"They were looking for instant gratification, instead of a lifelong commitment," added Peter.

"Oorgh," exclaimed Celia, "like bonobo chimpanzees!"

"Very much so," Peter agreed, "and this attitude was reinforced by a lot of the programmes on TV, and in the other media. It was very difficult for Christian parents to stop their children being corrupted.

"But when the Revival hit, people suddenly seemed to realise that they were meant to be spiritual beings instead of animals, and they just poured into the churches, seeking forgiveness and new life. Most of them hadn't been aware that they'd been breaking the third commandment several times every day, and a lot of them didn't realise they had been breaking the seventh commandment.

"There were meetings every night in all the churches. It was tremendously exciting! People used to fall on the floor without hurting themselves as they met God, and hundreds, probably thousands, were healed of every conceivable illness. It went on and on for months. Absomagnous!"

8

Celia thought Cambridge was wondrificent. It was October 2031, and she was now eighteen years old. The excitement she had felt about coming here to study zoology and molecular biology was still with her, even though lectures had already begun.

She had told some of the other students who were fast becoming her friends, that she wanted to walk back, pushing her bike alone to Girton College, where they were provided with accommodation and meals. It was a long walk — further than she had thought, and she decided that cycling would definitely be the preferred mode of travel to and from the university buildings in future.

She reminded herself of the lecturers' and professors' names: Miss Cassidy; Mr Strutt; Mr Fenwick; Prof. Rymer; Prof. Blair. They all seemed incredibly brainy, and they joined the students each morning at quarter to nine to pray.

Mr Strutt's words that morning, which she had found particularly inspiring, came to mind: "Our gracious Heavenly Father, during our time of vacation we have looked at Your world with eyes renewed in wonder. We praise You afresh for the beautiful complexity of Your creation. Help us as we examine parts of it in greater detail to retain our admiration and worship of You, the great Creator."

Celia's room was next to that of Beth, a tall blonde who was reading English.

They agreed to wedge their doors open for a while, at least while they were getting to know each other. The Yale locks would slam shut if they were careless, but they moved a button into position to prevent this.

"Doesn't it get a bit boring after a while, doing nothing but English?" Celia asked, hovering on Beth's threshold before they each settled down with their books and computers after lunch, to follow up the morning's lectures

"Oh no," Beth assured her, "there's Old English and Middle English as well. I quite enjoy studying the development of language."

"As a matter of fact, so would I," said Celia. "Our German teacher used to talk about it every now and then, and I was fascinated. He told us that 'Pfeffer' became English 'pepper' because the English word was brought over by the Anglo-Saxons before the second German soundshift took hold across the German-speaking states of that time."

Celia came further into the room and sat on Beth's bed in response to her new friend's wave in that direction.

"Sounds fascinating," commented Beth, "go on."

"He even told us a bit about Indo-European or Indo-Germanic. He said that philologists believe that even words like 'tooth', German 'Zahn', and 'dentist' (Latin 'dens, dentis' meaning 'tooth') derive from the same Indo-Germanic word, something like 'danth, danthus'."

"Go on," said Beth, keenly attentive, "can you explain how the words developed?"

"Er, the 'd' of the Latin became 't' in old Germanic, and remained 't' in English. In German the ending dropped away, first leaving 'tahn', which then developed into 'Zahn', through the second German soundshift. The English word 'tooth' went from 'tanth', then the 'n' dropped out, with lengthening of the preceding vowel, becoming 'tahth', and then 'tooth'."

"Oh! That was prima! I wish we had had a teacher like that at our school! You must tell me some more examples like that when we have some time to spare."

Celia noticed that Beth, who would be considered by many people to be pretty in a somewhat insipid way, looked very much prettier when she talked about something she liked or found interesting.

Celia knew that she herself was not exactly pretty, but she also knew that she had attractive eyes.

Evening dinner was at seven, preceded by a bell which was rung a quarter of an hour before, so that students could change into something at least slightly more formal than their daywear.

Celia considered this a waste of time, but she swallowed her objections and changed into a beige, body-hugging dress. It transformed her appearance, for it emphasised her charm and a certain beauty.

Beth had donned a pale blue dress which was a lighter shade than her eyes, but nevertheless brought out their colour. The two young women caught up with Emma and Joanna from the rooms opposite as they went downstairs to dinner.

The whole of Girton College seemed rather overpowering to Celia, who had little experience of older buildings. Virtually everything in Cartford dated from no earlier than the 1950s.

The dining hall was even more impressive. The vaulted ceiling looked to be about fourteen metres high, and the wooden-panelled walls bore large, ornately-framed portraits of women whose presence in Girton was not to be forgotten.

The students sat at tables set for ten places, and the Super[intendent] sat with some dons and professors and one invited student at a table on a raised dais, known as the "high table".

Celia felt ravenously hungry, but she was glad to discover that there was enough food for everyone, with even a little extra available for those who wanted it.

Like the other colleges of the university, Girton was for one gender only. There had in the past been a time when they were mixed, but eventually it was decided that the undergraduates worked more effectively at their studies when they restricted their socialising with the other gender to appropriate times.

This arrangement was very acceptable to Celia, who realised that things would have been considerably more disruptive and noisier here if male students had had free access. She was in no hurry to find a boyfriend. There had been Jamie, a dark-haired boy whom she loved for several years at school with the love of a devoted spaniel, although he was unaware of her adoration.

But unfortunately, although at first, when she was eleven and he was twelve, he had been about five centimetres taller, by the time she was fifteen and he sixteen, he had stopped growing, and she was six centimetres taller than he was. Her devotion had waned rapidly, and her interest had turned to Bob, a tall, blond lad whom she considered very good looking.

He was studying at a sixth-form college, but earned himself some money helping at a local farm stores market. They had begun chatting to each other when Celia was doing some shopping sometimes for her mother, then their friendship progressed a little further when Bob started to attend the youth group at Celia's church.

However, Bob decided to enlist as a volunteer in the army. The British army uniform was made of a very thick material, and it was spring when Bob came home on his first leave. The weather had turned suddenly warm, and during their visit to the cinema Celia discovered that her handsome boyfriend was not interested in deodorants. The stale perspiration lurking in the uniform was horribly overpowering, so that Celia could hardly wait to get out into the fresh air.

Bob found it difficult to understand why Celia was subsequently always too busy to accept any invitations.

Since that time her male friends had found her inexplicably uninterested.

Celia spent the evening working with her lap-top computer. The new work was amazingly exhilarating, and she passed two hours of great enjoyment. But suddenly there was a sharp pain in her abdomen.

It was so severe that she stretched out on her bed, trying to relax the painful area. She had had these pains quite frequently before, but all the tests to find out what was causing them had proved inconclusive — none of the doctors or consultants had been able to find anything wrong.

Eventually Celia decided to settle down for the night, at which point Beth returned from her evening out with some new friends.

Celia's door was open, so she strolled in for a chat.

"Isn't it a bit early to be going to bed?" she queried, kicking off her shoes and sinking onto a chair which had wooden arms, but was provided with comfortable padding as well as being ergonomically designed.

"I get a nasty pain in my tum every so often," Celia explained, as she lay on her bed, wrapped in a pale pink bathrobe. "At first my doctor back home thought it might be my appendix, then he thought it might be gallstones, but they couldn't find anything wrong with me when they examined me. I had every test in the book, I think."

"Oh, I hope it's nothing *really* serious," said Beth with concern in her voice. "Why don't you get your prayer group to pray for you tomorrow morning?"

"Yes, I think I will. The pain's gone now, but I'll go to bed anyway."

The two young women wished each other goodnight, Celia switched off her bedside light, and snuggled down to pray.

Next morning, towards the end of the prayer time in an ante-room of Laboratory No. 14, Celia followed Beth's advice and asked for prayer. As everyone turned their gaze upon her, she noticed Professor Rymer, who was looking at her very strangely. The thought "as if he had seen a ghost" came to mind; but now they were praying. For several minutes she felt bathed in the love of God. Then the prayer time ended, and everyone began moving away to their lectures.

Professor Rymer came striding across to speak to Celia. "Excuse me, are you related to Edith Owen? The family resemblance is so strong, I'm sure you must be!" he declared, with a warmth that seemed to be somewhat at variance with the apparent mixture of emotions in his face that he was attempting to control. His eyes, which were an unusually dark shade of blue, had a piercing quality. Celia thought he looked rather young to be a professor. Maybe in his forties.

"Yes, she's my aunt," she replied, wondering where this might lead.

"We were friends when she was a student," the professor explained. "It would be nice to get in touch again. D'you have her address or phone number?"

He pushed back a lock of dark, almost black hair from his forehead as he spoke, which made him look even younger.

"I haven't seen Auntie Edith for years, but I can give you the details of where she *was* living, if you like, and you can find out if she's still there."

Professor Rymer expressed his gratitude, and Celia promised to bring her aunt's details next morning.

Next day, however, it was not long after Celia had supplied the professor with her aunt's address and telephone number, and was on her way to lectures, when she suddenly doubled up again with pain.

Everyone was dumbfounded to see that she had apparently not been healed, in spite of their prayer the previous morning. She was taken to a small room where she could lie quietly and where a nurse was available for emergencies.

Celia explained that it had not so far been possible to find anything wrong with her.

The nurse looked at her rather sceptically. Yet it seemed a little early in the term for someone to be wanting time off from lectures. She checked Celia's blood pressure. Normal. Her pulse rate was a little faster than normal, but not unduly so.

As Celia was trying to convince the nurse that she wasn't joking, there was a knock at the door.

One of the secretarial staff put his head around the door and asked whether Percelia Prentis was in the room. There was an urgent message asking her to come to the Princess Alexandra Hospital in Cartford, where her aunt Edith was seriously ill. The doctors thought it might help her recovery if Miss Prentis could come to the hospital as soon as possible.

9

It was gallstones. Edith had been neglecting her health for many years, eating the wrong foods: sometimes gorging nothing but cream doughnuts and chocolate gateau; at other times eating very little, until her digestive system had been unable to cope.

After suffering repeated bouts of excruciating abdominal pain, she had finally been taken to hospital in Cartford.

As soon as she had been admitted and allocated a bed, Edith had asked for a message to be sent to her niece, Percelia Prentis, at Cambridge University, asking her to come as soon as possible. She assumed there was a possibility that she might not survive the operation; she *had* to see Celia again before that eventuality.

The ward sister had agreed to have the message relayed to Cambridge.

It was explained to Edith that her consent was needed for the medical staff to be allowed to take any measures during the operation which were considered necessary to save her life, possibly including the removal of any other diseased organ.

Edith had been reflecting on this possibility for perhaps ten minutes, when she was suddenly seized with terror. 'Percelia is part of me,' she said to herself. 'If I die, can she go on living?'

"Could I see the Protestant Chaplain, please?" she asked a nurse who was passing her bed.

"I don't know," she replied. "I'll send someone to find out for you."

"Oh, *please* find him or her quickly!" Edith pleaded desperately.

The nurse became more sympathetic. She drew closer and stroked Edith's hot forehead. "I'll see what I can do," she said gently, and went to pass on the message.

Edith lay there shaking with fear, and was still trembling when the Reverend Paul Kellard arrived at her bedside.

"Hallo, my dear," he said softly, bending over her tenderly. "How can I help you?" He looked about thirty-five, and his green eyes had an understanding expression.

"I've got something to confess," Edith whispered, barely audibly. "Do you hear confessions, and keep them completely confidential?"

"That's right," the Chaplain answered cheerfully, "it's part of my job, if that's what people want."

He proceeded to draw the curtains around the bed, even though the bed next to Edith's was unoccupied, and the women in the other two beds opposite seemed to be asleep.

"My name's Paul Kellard," he said quietly, as he sat down beside the bed, "I believe you're Edith. Is that right?"

She confirmed that he was correct about the name, and continued, "I've been trying to hide something that happened eighteen years ago, but now there's just a chance I might die on the operating table, I'm scared!"

"What are you afraid of?"

"When I was a student, and had almost finished doing my Education Diploma course, I let a friend of mine, who was doing research at Cambridge, use me in an experiment. He knew that human cloning was illegal, but he believed he could do it, so he wanted to see if his technique would work," Edith whispered. "He took some of my cells and did some work on them — I don't really know what it involved — and then he finally inserted one which was as viable as a normal fertilised egg into my womb . . . I carried the baby to full term. She was born in Scotland during the year before I started teaching."

"And did you bring her up yourself?"

"No," Edith admitted shamefacedly, "I thought she would be better off if she were adopted, hopefully by a mother and father who would love her."

"That sounds like a wise plan," Paul commented approvingly.

"But I think I made it more complicated than necessary. I wanted to keep in touch with the baby, and watch her grow up. So I concocted a story about my non-existent sister as being the mother. I told the adoption people that Celia's parents had died in a fire in Australia; she had been found in the garden by Aboriginals, and I had brought her back to Britain."

"So you called her Celia," said Paul thoughtfully. "Any particular reason for the choice?"

At that moment the curtain was pulled slightly aside, and a nurse peeped in cautiously.

"Sorry to disturb you," she said apologetically, "there's a visitor for Miss Owen."

"Oh, is it Celia?" Edith asked excitedly. "Let her come in please!"

As she came in through the folds of curtain, Edith uttered a murmur of joy, whilst the Chaplain stared in wonder at this younger, healthy version of the woman he had just been talking to.

Celia felt a deep wave of pity for her aunt as she lay there looking so ill. Her face, as well as her body, had become gaunt as a result of continual vomiting.

"I got your message," she said, coming close to the bedside and taking her aunt's hand in hers. Then she bent over and gave her a little kiss on the cheek.

"Thank you for coming, dear," Edith said, managing a wan smile.

As soon as Paul Kellard had been introduced, he went and tracked down the ward sister, insisting that Edith be moved to a private room on her own. "It's important for her recovery," he told her. "She must have sufficient privacy to be able to speak to me in confidence, even if it's just for an hour or two."

Edith's bed was wheeled along several corridors and into a small room reserved for isolation cases. There was a wash basin against one of the walls.

Edith wanted her niece to hear what she had been telling the Chaplain, so Celia and Paul Kellard seated themselves on each side of the bed.

"Brace yourself for the truth at last!" Edith said grimly, looking at Celia. "D'you remember saying you would find out the truth one day? Well, that day has arrived."

Celia stiffened, and there was alarm as well as suspense visible in her large, widened eyes. As Edith related the story of the cloning, Celia turned pale, then deathly white. She slid to the floor and lay still.

"She's fainted," Paul said in concern, hastening to pour her a glass of water. Having gone down onto one knee, he lifted the young woman's head gently, and held the glass to her lips.

A faint moaning was heard, then her eyes opened and began to roll around vacantly. After a few minutes, however, she began to breathe heavily as she regained consciousness. She took a few sips of water, and as her eyes were again able to focus, she fixed them on Edith as she sat up.

"So you're more like my mother than my aunt!" she declared, with a hint of bitterness and contempt. "Was it really necessary to invent all those lies?"

"I'm really sorry about all that!" Edith said in a small voice. "I didn't know how else I could watch you grow up. You're a part of me, you know."

"Well, there seems to be some truth in that! It must have been *your* pains I've been going through for the last few months. What've you got — gallstones?"

Edith's eyes widened in dismay. "Oh dear, that confirms what I'm worried about," she said unevenly, looking at the Chaplain.

He responded: "I'm still not at all sure what it is you're worried about."

"Celia and I share a body, in a way. Do we share a soul? If I die, will I be stuck in limbo until she dies? And will we join up as one soul when we're both dead?"

10

Professor Jonathan Rymer decided to cancel the afternoon's tutorial. The previous evening he had not had time to try phoning Edith, so he had tried when he had some free time before lunch. He guessed he would hear the answermachine, but he had not anticipated hearing: "You may be able to contact Edith Owen in Ward Fourteen, Princess Alexandra Hospital, Cartford. The number is: 01279 438666."

There was not a great deal of traffic on the motorway. Probably thanks to the much-improved network of public transport trains, buses and trams, he thought, compared with the situation that had existed about twenty years previously. And the trees and shrubs which had been planted on the central reservation even added a touch of beauty to the road. It had been an exceptionally boring and unattractive motorway many years before, when he was a young man enjoying the delights of driving, but fortunately successive governments had provided paid work, such as this planting, to those who had been unemployed.

Jonathan's MG covered the distance comfortably in about three quarters of an hour. He was asked to wait in a day room, as Miss Owen was having an important discussion with the Chaplain and a visitor.

In the small isolation room Paul Kellard had just prayed for wisdom to answer Edith's questions, when a nurse tentatively put her head round the door to ask whether another visitor, a Professor Rymer, would be welcome.

"Can you give us about ten minutes?" Paul asked. "I think Miss Owen would be happy to see another visitor by then."

The nurse withdrew, and reflectively Paul rubbed his chin, which was strong, Celia thought, making him look like an athlete. And his honey-coloured hair gave him a Scandinavian appearance.

"Firstly, I must ask Celia something," he said slowly. "Are you a Christian, Celia? Do you know Jesus in a personal way as your Saviour and Lord?"

She smiled. "I've known him since I was six," she said, "and I rededicated myself to him last year."

"I suppose you've been baptised?"

"Oh yes, and by immersion," she confirmed, smiling again.

"In that case I'm sure there's no problem," said Paul, looking at Edith encouragingly. "When a person is conceived and born in the normal way, he or she still needs to be spiritually reborn, through Jesus. Although Celia was not conceived in the normal way, her spiritual rebirth means that there's no doubt about her individuality. She's a separate person from you, Edith, adopted into God's family as His child."

The sound emitted by Edith on hearing these words was a kind of sigh, but also a gasp, of relief at the release of long pent-up worry and dread.

Then she said, "I'm glad you need have no fear of being stuck in limbo, Celia," and achieved a slight smile. "Now I think I'd better have a few minutes alone with the Chaplain."

Celia bent over the sick woman. "You may be the closest thing I've got to a biological mother, but I suppose it has to be kept a secret?"

Edith nodded.

Celia continued, "In that case, I'll still call you Auntie Edith. I hope the operation goes well." She gave her "aunt" a farewell kiss, and left her with Paul Kellard.

Edith said, "I think it's time I made a real commitment to God. I professed a belief many years ago, during the Great Revival, but it was only superficial, really. Will you help me make it real and deep, please?"

Paul took a small New Testament out of the breast pocket of his jacket, and read some verses to her, finishing with Revelation Chapter 3, verse 20: "Here I am! [says Jesus] I stand at the door and knock. If anyone hears my voice and opens the door, I will go in and eat with him, and he with me."

He explained that it referred to the door of one's heart. He then led her in a prayer of confession, asking for forgiveness for every sin, after which she received Jesus as her Saviour, and dedicated herself to Him.

There had been an opening and closing of the door of the small hospital room during the last prayer, and now a nurse appeared, announcing that it was time for Edith to be prepared for the operation.

"But there's another visitor waiting!" she objected. "Can't I see him for a few minutes?"

"No, I'm afraid not. We've given you ten minutes over time already. He'll just have to wait till later."

"You *will* tell him so, won't you?" said Edith, realising that she couldn't delay things any longer.

"Yes, we'll explain the position to him, don't worry," the nurse replied coolly, at which point the Chaplain took his leave.

Professor Rymer was not at all happy to be told that he would have to wait until after the operation to see Edith. He did not intend to waste time hanging about at the hospital, so he was about to return home to his house in Cambridge without further delay, when he saw Celia approaching.

"Hallo again, Prof. Rymer," she said, "I gather you weren't able to see my aunt after all."

"No, I was not," he replied grimly, "I'm just about to go home."

"Are you sure you want to go straight home?" Celia asked. "My parents live here in Cartford, and I'm sure they'd be happy to meet an old friend of Auntie Edith's. You could even stay the night — or at least enjoy a meal with us. My mother's a very good cook."

Prof. Rymer looked at the young woman thoughtfully. "Well, that sounds like an inviting offer. And if I stay overnight, I can drive you back to Cambridge in the morning. How's that?"

Celia thought it sounded splendiferous, so she received a joyful welcome on the telephone from June, who was delighted that her daughter would be making an unexpected visit home, and the professor would also be very welcome.

As neither of them had had any lunch, they stopped for a sandwich and a cup of coffee in the cafeteria.

Celia thought her mother would be home by now. June Prentis worked as a receptionist at the local clinic, where four doctors usually held their surgeries, and at least one nurse was in attendance. Her hours were from nine a.m. until two, which had been ideal while Celia was at school, and was still very convenient.

Professor Rymer was about to pop into the hospital shop to buy a toothbrush before leaving, when Celia forestalled him.

"My mother always keeps a few new toothbrushes handy, in case of unexpected visitors," she said, with a smile.

"Your mother is obviously a very hospitable lady," the professor remarked.

11

It was not far to drive from the hospital to Celia's home in the neighbourhood called "Deer Park". Although it was now October, there were still a great many roses blooming in the open front gardens of many of the houses, behind neat lawns, some planted with trees.

"I like the variety of the designs of the houses," Prof. Rymer remarked as they pulled to a stop where Celia indicated. "Have you always lived here?"

"Yes, since I was a baby," she replied, stifling the desire to add, "although I was born in Australia."

She was spared any further awkward thoughts by the front door opening. Her mother had seen the car as it arrived on the road outside, and came out to hug and kiss her daughter.

"What a lovely surprise to have you home!" she enthused. "Even if it wasn't a very pleasant occasion. And you're Professor Rymer, is that right?"

Jonathan shook her hand warmly, and they went indoors, while June asked Celia about Auntie Edith's operation.

"I don't really know," Celia replied. "I think they were going to operate soon after we left."

David had made a built-in bench seat in the kitchen, which fitted neatly between a worktop unit and the door to the entrance hall. He had also made a table of the same length, finished on the top with the same heat-resistant plastic as the other worktops, having a subtle two-tone beige floral design. The result was attractive enough to make the use of a tablecloth unnecessary.

June had been busy since receiving the phone call and arriving home from work. She had succeeded in preparing the spare room for the visitor as well as putting clean bedlinen on her daughter's bed, and had also made a chicken and mushroom pie.

Celia, who was sitting on the bench seat, agreed with the professor that the pie, which was accompanied by butter-fried potatoes and broccoli, was really delicious.

June sat at the end of the table, and David next to Jonathan.

"Well, I'm glad you and Auntie Edith are reconciled," said David to Celia with satisfaction. Then he turned to Jonathan. "They had some sort of disagreement when Celia was about fourteen, and hadn't seen each other since."

To his daughter he said approvingly, "I'm glad you decided to bury the hatchet, and went to see her."

"Well, I was told she was seriously ill, and wanted to see me," Celia explained. "I couldn't just brush her aside, could I? I've continued to pray for her all this time."

"And by doing so, you may have helped to save her life," commented June. She looked at the professor, "I don't suppose you know someone was trying to kill Edith about ten years ago?"

Jonathan's face changed instantly. He looked shocked and genuinely concerned. "What happened?" he asked, laying his fork back on the plate.

David told him the story of how Edith had discovered that the brakes of her car had been cut.

"The AA man said she must have a guardian angel," added June. "And I believe it was because Celia was praying for her."

"Were there any more attempts on her life?" asked Jonathan.

"Not as far as we know," said David, "but of course, God has an infinite number of ways of protecting people in response to His children's prayers."

Celia noticed that the professor's face, which had lost its colour at the mention of the attempt to kill Auntie Edith, was still just as pale. It seemed to her rather surprising that the news should have such an effect on him.

"May I ask how you and Edith got to know each other?" June asked. "Were you at Exeter University when she was there?"

"No, I wasn't at Exeter. We met at a student congress in Loughborough one year. She came to Cambridge a few times, but once she started teaching, we lost contact."

They enjoyed a dessert of peaches and icecream, followed by coffee in the lounge.

Celia's father insisted on washing the dishes, and wouldn't allow his daughter to dry them, so that she could sit and enjoy chatting to her mother and professor. David was of the opinion that dishwashers were a waste of electricity and water, regardless of the fact that they had had some solar panels installed in the roof — an amenity which reduced their electricity bill considerably.

Celia was doubly glad that Prof. Rymer had agreed to come to her home instead of driving straight back to Cambridge. Not only was it interesting to learn something about his relationship with Auntie Edith;

more importantly for the moment, she was able to sit back and listen most of the time, as her parents chatted to him. She was still trying to come to terms with what her aunt/mother had told her, and she would have found it an intolerable strain to converse as if everything were still as it had been until today.

Professor Rymer had got the impression that Cartford had been well designed.

"Yes," David agreed. "It was designed just after the Second World War, with four main sections, and quite a lot of neighbourhoods with their own shopping centre, their own primary schools intended to be within walking distance for every child, and eight secondary schools, likewise within walking distance.

"And the plan included a lot of green areas, keeping old trees and bushes."

"Yes, I noticed the green areas," said the professor approvingly. "And there's a great deal of variety in the designs of the houses. Some of them are very attractive."

"Yes, that's another thing we appreciate," said June. "Unfortunately there was quite a bit of filling in of some of the green areas during the 1980s," she added sadly.

After an enjoyable breakfast next morning, Celia

telephoned the hospital.

"They said the operation had gone well, and she's had a reasonably comfortable night," she reported to her mother and Prof. Rymer.

During the drive back to Cambridge the professor asked Celia about her choice of subjects for study.

"As I remember, your aunt Edith was very good at languages. She studied French and German, didn't she?"

"That's right, and that's what she teaches."

"Well, you look so much like her, I would have thought you had inherited some of the same genes from someone."

It had been raining since they had joined the motorway, and now the rain was swishing across the road in torrents, blown by strong gusts of wind. Jonathan increased the speed of the windscreen wipers as Celia answered:

"I *am* very good at languages, as a matter of fact, but I'm also very interested in biology and zoology. I had a really good biology teacher. He was enthusiastic about the way God had created everything . . . so am I. The more I learn about the creatures and plants He created, the more I admire Him!

"I decided to choose those subjects, with the idea

that if I can't find any way of earning my living through them, I can do translation work, using my specialised knowledge of the vocabulary."

"Mm-m — it sounds as if you would be a splendiferous translator!" the professor commented with a smile.

When he heard that she was in Girton College, he wondered whether it was still as cold as ever.

"I had one or two friends in Girton, when it was a mixed college," he said. "They were always complaining how cold it was most of the year — and the facilities were abysmal! On one floor there were only three toilets for twenty students. Is it any better now?"

"Oh yes, the windows on the accommodation floors have all been renewed and double glazed, and the decorative old windows on the ground floor have been fitted with secondary glazing, so it's reasonably warm. And there are eight toilets for twenty students on my floor, at least. I suppose it's the same on the other floors. We've got six showers and three baths on our floor, which isn't bad."

"Well! What an improvement! A pity it took so long to get it done!"

They arrived back at the Zoology Department at about ten o'clock that morning, Jonathan having had to keep his speed down somewhat, as visibility was impaired through the heavy rain.

He was taken aback, when he went to his room, to find a message on his screen: *Your mother has had a heart attack. She is in St Theresa's Hospital, Waterford.*

Another trip to a hospital. 'I hope this isn't becoming a habit!' he said to himself.

His mother had moved to Waterford, in Ireland, a few years previously, so as to be near his sister Priscilla, whose husband was Irish, and worked in Waterford.

'I was looking forward to seeing Edith again,' he thought, between giving instructions for the students to work on in his absence for a few days, and making arrangements for his flight to Dublin.

12

Jonathan's mother was sitting propped up against pillows when he located her in St Theresa's Hospital. She looked reasonably well, and somewhat younger than her sixty-five years. Her hair had only a few locks of grey among the dark brown, and her face, which was oval and always ready to smile, had hardly a wrinkle. It now lit up in a very attractive smile as she saw her son.

He bent over her, giving her a fond kiss as he presented her with a bouquet of red roses.

As she was beginning to thank him effusively, he joked: "What's the idea of having a heart attack? It was just an excuse for getting me to come over the Irish Sea, wasn't it?"

Her laugh was melodious. "I obviously don't look very ill then, if that's what you think! But, excuse or not, don't you think it's high time you came over to see me? D'you realise I haven't seen you since last Christmas?!"

Jonathan was apologetic, and was just attempting to explain that the work always involved so many challenging extra seminars, when his sister Priscilla arrived.

"Long time no see," she commented.

"Hallo Prissles," Jonathan said fondly, giving her a hug and a kiss. "Why don't you come over to Cambridge sometime?"

They exchanged excuses and news. Jonathan was persuaded to stay with Priscilla and her family for a few days until he could be sure that their mother was making good progress.

It was while he was reading the *Irish Times* two mornings later, after his sister's husband Michael had left for work, and their two children had gone to school, and while Priscilla herself was making last-minute preparations for the evening meal before setting out for her part-time job in the local library, that Jonathan noticed an item in the international section, headed 'News in Brief':

> Two former drug barons, Manuel Ortiz
> and Umberto Rodriguez, escaped from
> prison in Sogamoso yesterday. They had
> been serving a life sentence for murder.
> Interpol are seriously concerned that

they be recaptured in the next few days,

with their efforts concentrated on the

United Kingdom.

Jonathan's hands shook as he put the paper down on the coffee table by the sofa where he was sitting. His thoughts were racing.

Finding his sister in the kitchen, he announced, to her disbelief, "I'm sorry, Prissles, I've got to go back to Cambridge. Tell Mum I'm sorry I can't stay any longer. I must try to get the next flight back, or go by ferry if necessary."

"But I'm just . . ." Priscilla began.

"Sorry, I must pack my things and go. I'll make sure everything's locked up before I go." He grabbed her and gave her a hug and a kiss. "Thanks for having me. Cheers."

He picked up the phone and ordered a taxi, then raced upstairs to collect his belongings together.

Now it was time for his sister to leave for work. "OK Jonathan," she shouted. "Take care, and don't leave it so long next time! Cheers!"

He heard the front door slam shut, and she was gone.

The taxi driver looked at him with a wry grin. "I

wouldn't really mind taking you to Dublin Airport, but I don't really want to rob you. I take it you don't know there's an airport here, just outside Waterford! Where d'you want to fly to, may I ask?"

"London."

"Well, I'm pretty sure there are flights to London from there. D'you want to try them?"

Jonathan had never taken much notice of the signs pointing to Waterford Airport; he had always assumed that it was used for small, private planes operating within Ireland. But he now thought there might be more chance of an empty seat on a plane from a smaller airport, so he accepted the offer gratefully.

London flights were to London Stansted only. So much the better, he thought, on hearing that there were no flights to London Heathrow. Stansted was just off the motorway between Cambridge and Cartford.

Jonathan used a hired car to get to Princess Alexandra Hospital, Cartford, and found that Edith was doing well after the operation, with no problems. She was back in Ward Fourteen.

He was able to find some acceptable flowers in the hospital shop, which he used as a shield to hide his face.

"Ooh!" she exclaimed, as he suddenly appeared

from behind the bouquet. Then, recognising him, "What kept you?"

"I had to make a little trip to Ireland," he replied with a wry smile.

Edith appreciated the flowers. "They're beautiful!" she enthused, enjoying their fragrance.

She was on a drip, with a sign above her bed reading: NIL BY MOUTH.

"How well d'you feel?" he asked, a little less than sympathetically, she thought.

"You must get out of here soon," he said briskly, without waiting for a reply. "I heard about the attempt on your life that was made about ten years ago. I believe the men responsible are on the loose; I believe they've got out of jail."

Edith was scared, but not as terrified as she had been in the past. She guessed this was because of the assurance that God was with her. It meant that she was able to have a firm hope that He would help her.

"What do you know about that business?" she asked. "Who are the men you're talking about?"

Jonathan put his finger to his lips, and whispered, "They used to be drug barons, but were involved in other money-making schemes."

He paused reflectively. "I think I'd better wait till

you're stronger before telling you any more."

Having driven back to Cambridge, Jonathan went straight to the main police station.

Eventually, after a number of attempts to put him off, he was allowed to speak to Chief Superintendent Emmerson.

"Why should I believe you when you claim these men kidnapped and tortured you?" he asked, when he had listened attentively to Jonathan's story.

The professor showed him his right thumb. The nail was twisted and misshapen. "I suppose this isn't actual proof," he said. "But you're now looking at a thumb which had its nail torn out. They were trying to find out who else knew about my research at the time. I'm afraid I'm no hero when it comes to bearing pain. I told them the name of the one other person, and the university where she had been studying. I was lucky to survive. The police were pretty heavy-handed with their weapons when they raided the place. They knew these fellows were at the top of a powerful drugs cartel."

"I don't quite understand what they hoped to gain from holding you," the superintendent replied.

"They wanted me to give them details of the

cloning I had been doing with monkeys, chimps and gorillas. They wanted to use it to clone humans, and own the worldwide patent. It could have made them an extra fortune, on top of the drugs money."

"So now they're on the loose, you think you're in danger?"

"I haven't much doubt about it. And so is the woman I mentioned. They tried to kill her — at least, I presume they were behind it — about ten years ago. The brakes of her car were cut. I believe she reported it to the police . . . living in Bishops Stortford at the time, I think, though I'm not sure about that."

The superintendent leaned back in his chair thoughtfully. "Mm, well our two jailbreakers are not likely to bother to do their dirty work in person. We'll have to make a thorough check of the whole gang that Interpol have got on their files.

"Where is this woman — and what's her name, by the way?" he added.

"Edith Owen. She teaches in Cartford, but at the moment she's in hospital there. Just had an operation for gallstones."

"We'll arrange for you to stay at safe houses for a while, each of you at a different one. Get Miss Owen to send a message from the hospital to the school, saying she has to go away for three months to recuperate. We'll send a plain-clothes woman police officer to take her to a safe house."

"Oh, thanks very much," Jonathan responded with relief.

Emmerson got up and went to the door. "If you'd like to get yourself a cup of tea or coffee from the machine out here," he said, opening the door and pointing, "you can wait here while we get the details arranged. Then I think it might be useful for you to have a look at the files on the gang. Maybe you'll recognise some of them."

His guess was right. Jonathan recognised not only Ortiz and Rodriguez, but also five of the other men on the files.

"Very good," said the policewoman who had been showing him the files, "that could be really useful."

"I hope so," he replied grimly.

As soon as the arrangements were made, Jonathan was taken to a house in the wilds of Cambridgeshire, which was invisible from the road. He was driven by Jim, a plain-clothes policeman, in an unmarked police car up a narrow lane for about half a mile, then there was a right turn, another quarter of a mile, then up a narrow drive until they reached a farmhouse, which looked rather uncared-for, behind a high old brick wall.

Inside, it didn't look at all old. Everything was well decorated and well maintained. He was shown to a first-floor suite of rooms which had all the facilities and looked more comfortable than many a hotel room he had slept in.

Having assured himself of the location, he was then taken back to the police station at his request, so that he could use his own car to travel once more to Cartford.

It was now dark, and Jonathan was again grateful to those who had organised the planting of trees and shrubs on the central reservation of the motorway, so that there was very little dazzle effect from the cars travelling in the opposite direction.

He was surprised to find Celia at Edith's bedside. As it was Friday, she had decided to come home for the weekend, making use of the opportunity to visit her aunt.

This time he had no flowers, so Edith tactfully thanked him again for those he had brought earlier that day.

Jonathan remembered that Celia knew about the attempt on Edith's life, so he felt able to say to her,

"Your aunt is in danger, I'm afraid. The police believe the men who tried to kill her about ten years ago have got out of prison."

Celia's face showed her alarm and concern. "I'll ask God to put His angels in charge of her," she said, glancing at Edith with a certain satisfaction that now her aunt/mother was in a better position to benefit from His protection. Although she had not heard what Edith had said privately to Paul Kellard, Celia had an inner certainty that she had made a sincere commitment to Christ.

Jonathan addressed his next remarks to Edith. "You have to send a message to your school, telling them you're going away for three months to recuperate," he said in a low voice. "These are police instructions," he added.

Celia looked at her watch. "I'd better be going," she said, "Mum and Dad will want to have a chat before bedtime."

Edith expressed her sorrow that it would be at least three months before they would see each other again, and Celia left to catch a bus home.

"I hope they'll let you eat a bit of solid food tomorrow," Jonathan said, with concern audible in his voice.

"Oh, there's a good chance they will," she replied reassuringly.

"A policewoman in plain clothes, named 'Emma' is going to collect you sometime tomorrow and take you to a safe house," Jonathan explained. "I'll try to come and see you there, if they'll let me."

"Oh, I hope they will. It'll get a bit tedious being cut off like that for three months."

"I've been given accommodation in a safe house, too," Jonathan told her. "So maybe no one will find us. I hope to be able to catch up on my reading . . . it would be prima to read even half of the books I have on the shelf that I never got round to reading!"

He gave her a brief kiss on the cheek, and left.

As soon as he had gone, Edith asked whether the Chaplain was available, receiving the reply that she would be able to see him from nine o'clock the next morning.

Paul wasted no time responding to her request; he felt that this was an important part of his work — the patients were usually in their fifties or sixties, nearly always suffering from conditions that had been produced by unwise lifestyles in their youth before the Great Revival.

Edith explained to Paul in a low voice, that she was

to be taken to a safe house. He had been appearing at her bedside every day since she had made her commitment to Christ, giving her advice and booklets about the faith, including "Every Day with Jesus", which, he told her, was published every two months, and which she was finding most helpful.

"Paul," she said, "do you think you could pop in to see Celia before she goes back to Cambridge, and arrange to pass on any messages to her while I'm in purdah, please?"

"Mm, well, I can't manage it today, I'm afraid, but tomorrow afternoon may be possible. I'll try ringing her then."

"Oh, thank you so much," Edith replied warmly, "I won't feel quite so cut off if I can communicate that way."

"That's OK, I'll be happy to pass on your messages. But now that you're a Christian, you never need feel lonely again, you know. Jesus said, 'I am with you always, till the very end of the age'."

13

It seemed increasingly clear to Celia, as she walked through the cool evening air to the bus stop, that Prof. Rymer must have been the research student Auntie Edith had mentioned, who had persuaded her to co-operate with him in his cloning experiment. That would surely explain his interest in both of them: Auntie Edith and herself.

He also seemed to know quite a lot about those escaped prisoners, and why they were a threat to her "aunt".

As she reached the bus stop, Celia saw the bus approaching, and that it was the right number to take her homewards. There were about half a dozen people downstairs, so she had no difficulty finding somewhere to sit. Once she was seated, and the bus moved off again, her thoughts continued.

If what she suspected about Prof. Rymer were true, he would be the nearest person she had to being her biological father! It was a fascinating thought, but it revived the anger she had felt on first hearing that she was a replica of Auntie Edith. A replica. The memory of the anagram of her name surfaced once more. REPLICA E — replica of Edith! So that's what 'Percelia' really meant!

She struggled with her feelings of rage for several minutes. Then the thought of her aunt/mother's fear of the probable danger she was in rose up in her consciousness. Auntie Edith needed her prayers, not her anger.

She looked upwards, mentally passing through the upper deck and top of the bus, concentrating on the great Creator of the universe, who likes to be regarded as Father, and asked Him to put His angels in charge of Auntie Edith for the rest of the evening, night, and throughout the next day, so that no harm or hurt could be done to her during that time.

She had found that if she included the time factor, her faith for that time was complete and undoubting; a prerequisite for her prayers to be granted.

The pleasure that Celia's parents expressed at her unexpected trip home for the weekend soon turned to concern when their daughter told them about the escaped prisoners, and that the police believed they were responsible for the attempt on Auntie Edith's life.

Celia didn't mention Prof. Rymer in this context; she considered it to be probably best to wait to find out definitely whether her suspicions were founded on fact.

David and June immediately began to pray for Auntie Edith's safety, as soon as Celia had finished telling them the news. Then June added a prayer for the escapees:

"Father, please have mercy on those men who've escaped from prison. Please speak to them by Your Holy Spirit; remind them of the true things they've heard and read about Jesus. Please help them to receive Your forgiveness and salvation. In the name of Jesus, Amen."

"Amen!" David and Celia agreed.

Next day being Saturday, Celia was sorry that her friend Octavia was now a student at St Andrew's University. However, she enjoyed a long telephone chat with her, and fixed a weekend when they would both be home.

The weather had turned warmer, with autumn sunshine, so David and June took their daughter to Epping Forest for a walk in the woods among the fallen leaves.

The following day, Sunday, Celia enjoyed an inspiring morning at the local Pentecostal Church with her parents. The awareness of the presence of Jesus was almost tangible, as several elderly people were healed of physical and emotional problems that had developed through their use of drugs or alcohol when they were in their twenties and thirties.

Celia had intended returning to Cambridge soon after lunch, but as they were just finishing eating a delicious apple pie that June had made, the telephone rang. It was the hospital chaplain.

"Hallo Celia, Paul Kellard here."

She returned his greeting, a little surprised to hear his voice, but which she recognised at once: strong, deep and vibrant.

"I don't know what time you're planning to go back to Cambridge," he continued. "Can I see you for a few minutes before you go? It's about your aunt."

"I don't need to go for a few hours yet. You can speak to me here, at home, if you like."

"Right, I'll be with you in about ten minutes. See you soon."

"OK, bye."

After Paul had been introduced to Celia's parents and joined them in a cup of tea, David and June decided to go out for a walk, leaving the chaplain free to relay Edith's message.

"She still likes to keep the contact!" Celia remarked with a smile. "I'll be quite happy to receive messages from her, and help her in any way I can."

She explained how she used to feel as a girl growing up under the shadow, as it were, of this "aunt" who lied to her so often and so strangely.

"I think I'm beginning to understand, now, why she did it. It must have been a terrible strain for her," she said sympathetically.

"Are you going back by train?" Paul asked.

"Yes, I've got a return ticket."

"I'll drive you back, if you like, then I'll see which college you're in, in case I think it's safer to speak to you in person, rather than on the phone."

His suggestion sounded very appealing, so she accepted the offer gratefully.

There was no hurry, now that there was no train to catch, so they continued to chat, enjoying getting to know each other better.

June and David were a little surprised to see Paul's car still outside the house when they returned from their walk, but were quite happy to hear of the new arrangement.

They, too, liked chatting to this amiable young man over a cup of tea. He had quite a range of amusing stories in his repertoire, so they found him most entertaining, and were rather sorry when it was time for him and their daughter to set off.

Paul and Celia stopped for a meal at a service restaurant on the motorway, which was modelled on a German-style Raststätte.

They both appreciated the pleasant, welcoming layout, and also the wide variety of foods to choose from.

The staff consisted almost entirely of foreign students. Most were from Germany, but there were one or two from France. They were spending a year in the UK between studies, to improve their English skills.

When Paul and Celia had finished their main course, which they had selected from a self-service counter, the student who pushed the dessert trolley near to their table sounded German as he invited them to choose a sweet.

"Are you from Germany?" Paul asked.

"Yes, I am. I am here since one month," he said in a friendly manner.

"Are you staying near here?"

CHAPTER THIRTEEN

"Not too far. In Cartford," he replied.

"Oh, that's where I live," Celia told him.

"So do I," added Paul. "Have you found a church that you like?"

"We work only half a day on Sundays," he said, "and I am doing six weeks mornings, then it will be six weeks afternoons and evenings. I want to find a church in Cartford which has Sunday evening services."

"I'm fairly sure there's one in the south-west corner of Cartford," Paul said. "I think it's called Kingsmoor Community Church. That's where the revival started in Cartford, about twenty years before the Great Revival, I believe. The church kept growing so fast, they had to keep building extensions, and now I understand they persuade people to opt for the evening service if possible, so that there's enough room in the morning."

"Yes, you're right," Celia confirmed. "That's my parents' church, and mine when I'm home. But there's another big church along the main road from that one, in a shopping centre. It used to be a fast-food restaurant, but I believe it's now called the Church of the Messiah. It's possible that they have services in the evening — I've heard that they have trouble finding seats for everyone; their music group is so good."

The student beamed with pleasure as Celia wrote down the details for him. "Thank you very much. I will find one of these this evening."

He continued to smile as he served them with their choice of dessert.

As they drew into Cambridge, Paul suggested that it might be a wise precaution if, once she had pointed out where she was staying, he dropped her some distance away, leaving her to walk the rest.

"Your travel bag isn't very heavy, is it," he added.

Celia agreed that it was probably better to be safe than sorry, so she got out of the car about a hundred metres from the entrance to her college.

"Thanks again for the ride," she said with her attractive smile. "Let me know how Auntie Edith's getting on."

Paul promised to do so; they said their farewells, and Celia walked along the well-lit street to her college.

14 >

14

Edith was able to persuade Emma, the policewoman who took her to the safe house, that she needed a large number of books brought from her house in Bishops Stortford.

"All in a day's work," commented Emma cheerily as she took the list of books, and also promised to take Edith's indoor plants to her mother's in Rayleigh. Then she added, "Just as well you're back on solid food, isn't it?"

"It is indeed," Edith replied fervently. "I'll soon be eating normally again."

She had a suite of rooms at her disposal, including a small kitchen/dining room where she could prepare her own breakfast or order something from the kitchen downstairs. At other mealtimes there was a choice of cooked food which was brought to her suite.

Apart from her bedroom and bathroom, there was also a small lounge.

'Well,' she thought, 'it's certainly going to be no hardship living here for a few months!'

She was left to wait, however, until the next day for the books. Fortunately she had the small supply of booklets, and a New International Version of the Bible that the chaplain had given her, to keep occupied for a while.

Her thoughts turned, inevitably, to the question of how efficient those murderous jailbirds might be in finding their prey.

The windows appeared, from the outside, to be leaded with old rectangular small panes of glass, but Edith was comforted to see that the verticals were reinforced on the inside with strong metal bars. Perhaps it really was a "safe house".

* * * * * * *

Prof. Jonathan Rymer had likewise prevailed upon Jim, his guardian policeman, to fetch some books from his house in Cambridge. He guessed that the police had ways of doing this without attracting attention, but Jonathan was unable to extract the information from him.

He didn't pursue the matter unduly, however, for he was hoping for another favour. He wanted to see Edith, but realised that it would ruin the whole purpose of being given sanctuary in the safe house if he were to use his own car. It would have to be some kind of police van.

Jim, however, had plenty of other duties to claim his attention. "I'm not your nursemaid, you know," he replied with a grin, when the professor expressed his request.

"You'll have to wait till I've got a genuine reason for going over to that part of Essex," he said with a hint of sympathy. "Just be ready to leave everything at a few minutes' notice any time, and I'll take you." Then, as Jonathan was thanking him, he added, "But I'd better warn you — our vans are not very comfortable!"

Jonathan assured him that he would probably survive the trip, having lived through being in a certain South American country famous for its potholes!

Ten days later he was relieved that it was not the middle of the night when Jim found it possible to fit him into a drive to Linton.

"It won't be too much of a detour, even though Linton is in Cambridgeshire. It's not far from that part of Essex," he announced. "You can bring a cushion with you if you like!"

"I'm not that much of a wimp!" the professor

retorted genially.

He began to wish, however, as the white van bumped and jolted its way along the roads and lanes of the Essex countryside, that he *had* taken up the policeman's suggestion and brought a cushion.

After a two-hour journey, which seemed to Jonathan to have taken twice as long, Jim introduced him to the security guard at the door of Edith's safe house.

"It'll probably be a couple of hours before I can pick you up again," Jim called out as he hurried back to the van. "See you!"

The guard accompanied the professor to Edith's suite, but left them once he had confirmed that she knew him as a friend.

"Well, it's not such a bad life, this, is it?" Jonathan remarked as he walked in, looking around approvingly.

"No, I'm not complaining," she replied with a smile. "Would you like a cup of tea?"

"That's the best proposal I've heard for a long time. If you came here in a police van, you'll know what I mean!"

"Yes, I did, and I do," Edith said with a grimace as she went to boil the kettle for tea.

There were two comfortable armchairs in the small lounge, so the professor was glad to stretch back and relax. "This tea tastes wondrificent!" he enthused.

"My mother taught me how to make a good cup of tea. I suppose some people simply don't know how to do it."

"Did she teach you to cook, too?" Jonathan asked, glancing at his watch. It indicated half past four. "My guardian policeman said he wouldn't be back to pick me up for a couple of hours."

"Well, all my meals except breakfast are brought up to me. But I expect they can manage to find something for you if you're still here at six thirty."

"I suppose you're eating normally again now?" Seeing her nod, he continued, "You're certainly looking a lot better now than last time I saw you. I needed to look at Celia to remind myself how you used to look!"

"Yes . . ." Edith said thoughtfully, "I'm still waiting for an explanation of why someone was trying to kill me. Can you enlighten me?"

"I think so," Jonathan replied, swallowing hard. "In 2019 I was kidnapped and taken to Columbia. Those fellows I told you about, who were involved with drugs in a big way, were interested in cloning. They had discovered, maybe from articles in 'Nature', that I was experimenting with cloning chimps and gorillas, and it seems they got some information from a woman who did some cleaning in my private lab. She saw something on my computer which seemed to indicate that I might be trying to clone humans.

"They thought they could make even more money by patenting the technique worldwide. And from snatches of their conversation I guess they had some worse plans. But first, they wanted to make sure no one else knew about it."

At this point Jonathan leaned over to where Edith was sitting, and showed her his misshapen thumb.

"I wouldn't tell them anything at first . . . but by the time they had pulled out my thumbnail, I was babbling your name."

Edith's face changed, and set in a hard, frozen expression.

"What else did you tell them?" she demanded coldly.

"They said they would pull out the rest of my fingernails if I didn't give them some details about you. I told them the only thing I knew was that you had been a student at Exeter University."

Seeing the look on her face, he added, "I hoped that wouldn't be any help to them."

"Your hope was ill founded," she commented bitterly. "So it didn't matter to you that I might be murdered!"

"But it *did* matter! . . . I hope *you* never have to experience anything like that kind of torture!"

Edith stood up and walked to the door. Opening it, she said, "You obviously can't be called a friend any more. Perhaps the people downstairs will give you something to eat."

Jonathan stared at her in disbelief. It had never crossed his mind that she might react in this way. He had assumed she would understand how painful his ordeal had been. He went to the door in a daze, saying, "Oh, goodbye then."

Edith closed the door behind him as he went out, and walked over to the window. 'So that's the sort of fellow he is!' she thought. 'Betrays his friends under torture!'

15

The more she thought about the whole thing, the angrier Edith felt towards Jonathan. 'He has really messed up my life,' she thought bitterly. 'Because of him I have a daughter who has never been a real daughter — I've never been able to have a good relationship with her. She even seemed to hate me when she knew I was lying. And because of her I've never married.' She attempted to suppress a tiny voice somewhere inside which was trying to insinuate that the real reason she had never married was that she had never met a man whom she found as attractive as Jonathan.

'He betrayed me!' she repeated to herself. 'What real friend would do a thing like that?' Her thoughts continued to whirl around thus in her head throughout the rest of the evening.

* * * * * * *

In the meantime, Jonathan had descended the stairs slowly, almost in a trance. He had been only too well aware, especially since hearing about the attempt on Edith's life, that he had been responsible for putting her life in grave danger. But he had expected her to understand that heroes who can withstand severe torture are actually few and far between. Yet there was no escaping the fact that this was precisely what Edith did expect of him. A new thought came into his mind: 'She must have put you on a pedestal'!

He was surprised at the thought, but it made him feel even more dejected.

In response to his knock on the kitchen door it was opened by a young woman — young? He realised that he had at first glance categorised her thus, but then became aware that she was probably a few years older than himself. Expressions such as "farmer's daughter" or "milkmaid" surfaced in his mind, for she could best be described as "buxom", with long, curly hair which deserved the word "golden", and she was wearing a sleeveless top, despite the cool autumn weather.

However, Jonathan realised that it was not at all cool in this kitchen. There were some delectable-smelling wafts of air teasing his nostrils; several tempting kinds of food seemed to be simmering on the cooker.

"Hallo, come in," she said with a pleasant smile, shaking his hand, "I'm Cheryl. Our security guard, Michael, told us you were a friend of Edith's. Jonathan, isn't it?"

"Yes, I'm Jonathan Rymer."

"What can I do for you?"

"I'm afraid we've had a bit of a bust-up. She's very angry with me about something, and doesn't want to see me again."

"Oh, sorry to hear that. But excuse me for a moment, I have to let Michael know the position."

Cheryl went over to a telecommunications unit and got through to the security guard, explaining Jonathan's predicament.

"Of course, he can stay here with us, as long as necessary," she said. "OK."

She put down the receiver and indicated another door. "Come and meet my husband," she said, leading the way into their living-room.

The man sitting in an armchair watching television, who looked about five years older than himself, switched it off when he saw them enter, and got up.

"Jonathan and Edith have fallen out," Cheryl announced with equanimity, and turned to the professor. "This is my husband, Sam."

As soon as they had been introduced, Jonathan was invited to sit down and make himself at home while Cheryl served up the food.

Michael came down from his suite opposite Edith's, to collect his meal, while Sam carried Edith's tray upstairs.

There was no one else upstairs, so Cheryl, Sam and Jonathan sat round the large pine table in the kitchen to eat. Having joined in a prayer of thanks to God, Jonathan soon found himself expressing his appreciation to the woman who had cooked it. "Really delicious!" he enthused.

"I enjoy cooking," said Cheryl, swallowing rapidly to allow a smile.

"And enjoys eating!" added her husband.

"Speak for yourself, Mr Arbuckle!" she retorted.

"That's a bit of an exaggeration," remarked Jonathan, for Sam was only slightly rounder than his wife.

He began to wonder aloud whether Sam and Cheryl lived here on a regular basis.

"Yes," Sam answered. "Although we're both trained police officers, and could be called out in an emergency if there was no one sheltering here, we live here ostensibly like any other couple whose children are now at university."

"We provide bed and breakfast in a private sort of way, only to our friends, you know," added Cheryl.

"I see. And what does your husband do, ostensibly, for a living?"

"He has a job working at home with computers," she replied.

"May I ask where you get your food? D'you have to go shopping for it?" Jonathan asked.

"We have quite a big garden at the back of the house, where I grow a lot of vegetables," said Sam. "But Cheryl fetches the rest by horsecar from the village supermarket five miles away. Most of the food they sell is grown or produced locally."

"That's good. I'm glad the Government has put so many restrictions on the big supermarket chains that used to take most of the farmers' profits."

"Yes, they get a reasonable price nowadays, including for milk," said Cheryl with satisfaction.

"Who looks after the horse?" Jonathan queried.

"We share him with a farmer in the next village," replied Cheryl. "He's also a part-time police officer, available for emergencies, like ourselves. We take it in turns to use the horsecar, and, of course, to look after the horse. But we do have a Land-Rover that runs on rapeseed oil, and we can buy that from the same farmer."

"I've never actually ridden in a horsecar," Jonathan admitted. "I suppose it's all right in the rain — the roof juts out forward over the rear end of the horse, doesn't it?"

"That's right," said Sam, "the driver usually stays fairly dry when it's raining."

"And of course the droppings are excellent for the garden," Cheryl pointed out with a laugh.

"I suppose the horsecars are light enough for one horse to pull?" Jonathan wondered. "Are they made of fibreglass?"

"I believe so — something like that, anyway," said Sam. "They are certainly very light."

After the meal Cheryl made a pot of coffee while Sam loaded the dishwasher, and they returned to the living-room to drink it.

An impressive-looking grandfather clock standing in the corner began to strike seven as Jonathan was finishing his coffee.

"Good heavens — is that the time?!" he asked in astonishment.

"Yes it is. That clock keeps excellent time," Sam told him with a hint of pride.

"Jim — that's my guardian policeman — should have been here long ago to pick me up. I hope nothing's happened to him!"

"Don't worry," said Cheryl soothingly, "he's probably been called away on some emergency."

"You may be right," said Jonathan doubtfully, "but you must admit it's a bit worrying."

"If you're really worried, we can pray for him, if you like," Sam suggested.

The professor considered this an excellent proposal, so they prayed together for Jim's protection.

"If he doesn't arrive by ten thirty, he'll leave it till tomorrow," Sam remarked after the prayer.

"Tomorrow!" echoed Jonathan. "Where am I going to sleep, if that happens?"

"You can stay here with us," said Sam in a matter-of-fact tone. "We've got a spare bedroom, and there are two more suites on the second floor."

"Oh, that's very kind of you. But I don't need a suite! Though I'd appreciate a toothbrush."

"I'm sure the spare bedroom will be fine for you, if necessary," said Sam. "I'll see if I can locate Jim for you."

"And we *can* supply you with a new toothbrush!" declared Cheryl. "We often get people arriving here very unexpectedly — from their point of view as well as ours — so we always keep a stock of new toothbrushes."

The professor listened for what seemed to him a considerable time to police radio chitter-chatter and banter, as Sam endeavoured to find out the whereabouts of his guardian policeman. At last the news came through.

"His van broke down the other side of Linton. He's been taken home, and he'll pick you up sometime tomorrow."

16

Next morning Edith found solace in reading some of the gloomier psalms. They suited her mood well, except for the parts referring to her "enemies", where she would have benefited from an explanation: that Christians find it helpful to regard these as *spiritual* enemies.

Nevertheless, words such as "O God, You are my God, earnestly I seek You; my soul thirsts for You, my body longs for You, in a dry and weary land where there is no water", and "Listen to my prayer, O God, do not ignore my plea; hear me and answer me. My thoughts trouble me and I am distraught . . ." were somehow supportive.

In spite of all her negative thoughts throughout the previous evening, she had half-unconsciously been listening for the van which would take Jonathan back to his safe house. But she hadn't heard it. When she retired to bed, she assumed that the sound of the van's engine had simply not reached her.

It was almost eleven o'clock that morning when Edith heard the chugging of a vehicle approaching. From the window she could see the turning space at the front of the house, and she saw a white van draw up as she watched at the edge of the net curtains.

The man who got out seemed to be carrying a small sack.

A few minutes later there was a knock at her door. "Emma asked me to pass these on to you," said the man with a friendly smile.

He put his hand in the small sack and pulled out a large handful of letters.

"Are you Jim, by any chance?" Edith asked, as she accepted all the letters.

"That's my name," he responded cheerily.

"I suppose Jonathan got back all right yesterday evening?" she queried, half trying not to ask.

Jim looked at her in surprise. "Oh, didn't you know he spent the night here? I've just come to pick him up. The van broke down. I got it sorted this morning."

Edith made an attempt to cover up her embarrassment. "Oh . . . no. He must be friendly with the people downstairs," she faltered.

"Well, he's well and all's well! Cheers!" He turned

and made his way to the stairs.

Edith's spirits rose and blossomed with wonder as she saw that the huge bundle of letters consisted almost entirely of "Get Well" cards made and decorated by students of various ages from her school.

She spent the rest of the morning in incredulous enjoyment as she admired the multiplicity of colours and designs achieved by the children. Some of the greetings were in French, and some in German, with various and entertaining degrees of accuracy: from *Getten Sie Wohl* to *Bon sanité!.*

As she was beginning to wonder why the cards came to be transported by Jim, in the absence of Emma, she found a letter from Celia.

Dear Auntie Edith,

I hope you're feeling a lot better now, and are eating normally again.

University life is prima. I really enjoy the work, and the lecturers and professors are friendly as well as knowledgeable. Beth, the girl next door, and I are already really good friends.

Octavia has invited me to spend the half-term long weekend with her at St Andrew's. I can't wait to see her again!

Paul Kellard, the hospital Chaplain, has promised to take this letter, and any others that have come for you, to the police station, so that they can make sure you get them.

Many blessings,
Love
Celia. xx

* * * * * * *

Octavia could hardly contain her delight when Celia told her that she had managed to get a cheap flight to Edinburgh, so she would be coming after all! At first it had seemed that Mr and Mrs Prentis couldn't afford the air fare.

Celia received a government grant to cover her tuition fees, residential expenses, and a small allowance for books and computer equipment, but any other expenses were paid for by her parents.

The much-anticipated Friday arrived, and Octavia met her friend at the station in St Andrew's at 12.15.

"We'll be just in time for lunch, if we don't dawdle, Perce!" said Octavia, after a fond hug of welcome and expressions of delight at seeing each other again.

Celia had not brought very much luggage, and she

was wearing some warm clothes, including a water-proof anorak, after being urged to do so in the telephone conversations the two friends had engaged in more and more frequently as the long weekend drew near.

It was not far to walk from the station to Octavia's college, so they were in time for lunch. As they ate, sharing their latest news, Octavia broached the subject of her plans for the next couple of days.

"I didn't mention this before, in case your parents might disapprove," she said with a conspiratorial air. "Two of my friends, Duncan and Bruce, want us to go to the mountains of Glencoe tomorrow. We can go in Duncan's car, and they're going to bring some little tents and sleeping bags. You will come, won't you?"

Celia gazed at her friend reflectively. "It won't involve climbing mountains, will it? I'm not used to that at all!"

"Oh no, we'll just be walking, but I'm sure the views will be glorious!"

"And I might share a tent with you, but not with any males!" Celia said decisively. Then she added, "But I think it would be too cold to sleep in a tent."

"Oh, Duncan is used to walking on Scottish mountains, and he thinks his sleeping bags are warm enough."

"Well, it might be fun, but I'm not making any promises," Celia said in a warning tone. "And if the weather's bad, I'll stay in the car!"

"Oh, what a wet blanket you are!" laughed Octavia. "Can't you see the sunshine? I admit it's quite cold outside, but I can see blue sky!"

They enjoyed an afternoon stroll around the interesting parts of the town, some historic parts having an almost magical feel, Celia thought. The stones of the ruins seemed to hold their own mysterious story, waiting to be told if one could be quiet enough. 'This must be a wonderful place in the warmer months,' she said to herself.

To her friend she said, "You made a good choice, coming to St Andrew's. It's a prima place to study."

"I think so too," Octavia agreed. "The boys will bring some food tomorrow, but we'd better get some, too."

They found some shops with the kind of food they were looking for, including some 'butteries' — a kind of flat roll made with butter — a new experience for Celia.

Duncan and Bruce had arranged to meet at Rob Roy's, a favourite restaurant, at seven o'clock, so that they could get to know Celia.

Both young men were very tall, Duncan looking like a typical Scot, with his sandy-coloured hair and eyebrows and pale blue eyes, and Bruce giving the impression almost of a wrestler — a real heavyweight. He didn't look particularly Scottish, Celia thought, as she considered his fairly dark hair, which was nearly as dark as Octavia's, and brown eyes.

The restaurant seemed to be full of students, for the food was always good and prices affordable. However, they managed to find a suitable table.

As they were enjoying their meal, which came up to their expectations, Octavia told them what Celia's reaction had been to their plans, and the two young men exchanged meaningful glances.

Seeing this, Celia said, "You can find someone else if you like. I'm definitely not going to share a tent with either of you, and if the weather's bad, I'm not going hill-walking or mountain-walking!"

"OK," said Duncan in a pacifying tone, "we'll drive to Glencoe, but if the weather's bad we'll just drive around a bit, then come home. How's that?"

"Promise?"

"I promise," said Duncan solemnly.

"Are you a Christian?"

"Yes!"

Celia began to ask them questions about their faith, and they recounted their experiences of the reality of Jesus, including some highly personal incidents.

"I was helped as a child by reading C. S. Lewis's *Narnia* books, and then later by his adult books, especially *Mere Christianity*," added Bruce.

"They helped me, too," agreed Duncan, "and so did Colin Urquhart's books, and also *The Essential Book of Recipes for Good Living*, by a woman who was a lay preacher."

Listening to their thoughts and recollections, gradually Celia came to believe that they were both sincere Christians.

She had sometimes met people who made similar assertions, including dramatic conversions, but whose claims had subsequently proved to be hollow. But she had a feeling of certainty about the sincerity of Duncan and Bruce.

"OK, I'll come with you on the basis of your promise," she said at last.

17

It was a bright, crisp morning, with sunshine and a blue sky inviting Celia's admiration as she looked out to check the weather. She had been given permission to use the study bedroom of a student who had gone home for the weekend, in return for a small fee to cover laundry and breakfast, which Octavia had arranged to pay.

She had almost finished dressing when her old friend knocked and almost simultaneously put her head round the door.

"Oh good, you're up," Octavia observed brightly. "Lovely morning, isn't it?"

"Yes, it's beautiful. Have you finished your prayers?"

"I usually keep them short when I'm going out early, and hope there'll be a chance to pray sometime later in the day."

"Well, sometimes I do that, but just give me five minutes for a few basic prayers. I think I can find the way down to breakfast."

"OK, don't get carried away!" With that, Octavia left her friend alone to pray.

They had almost finished an enjoyable Scottish breakfast when a student came over to their table with the news that their two friends were waiting for them in the entrance hall, so they dashed upstairs to put on their warm waterproof gear and pack the food.

Duncan was in the driving seat of his Rover jetcon car, and the others each took turns sitting next to him, so that they could have a share of the best views.

Their route took them first through less picturesque countryside, while Duncan was careful to avoid the horseback riders and horsecars, to reach the motorway, then past Perth and continuing up the motorway towards Inverness until they turned off westwards into the Tay valley.

Now the views were really worth seeing, as they travelled on beside Loch Tay, with mountains on each side, and these now had a covering of sunlit snow.

"Why don't we stop here and have some lunch," suggested Bruce when they were near the end of the loch. They had stopped mid-morning for coffee at a pleasant little restaurant, and now Bruce was not the only one feeling hungry.

They discovered that, although it was now November, it was warm enough to sit on a groundsheet in a sunny spot in front of a rocky area, to eat their picnic.

It emerged that they had had similar thoughts: rolls which they had bought ready filled with a good variety of fillings.

"Mm-m," murmured Bruce appreciatively. "These rolls certainly taste good in the highland air! We should come here more often!"

The others agreed that the rolls were prima. Then the tastes diverged as they made their choice of fruit pies, doughnuts, or fresh fruit.

"What part of Scotland d'you come from, Bruce?" Celia asked, wondering whether he had grown up in this kind of scenery.

"Motherwell, Glasgow," he replied. "My home is not in an exactly scenic neighbourhood!" Then he added, "But I'm told it's a lot better than it used to be. The houses that people like my parents can afford are better designed and better built than they used to be when they were children, and there are a lot more gardens."

"What about you, Duncan?" Octavia asked, "I seem to remember that you come from the Dee valley. Is that right?"

"Aye, Banchory. It's a fine place to live. Except that it gets a bit crowded with tourists in the summer. Or folk from Aberdeen. It's a favourite place for them, as well."

"One of my grandmothers lives in the Dee valley," said Celia. "Ballater. But I don't remember it very well. I've only been there twice, and that was when I was quite small. But I remember a lovely garden to play in. There was a girl of my own age next door, and we had a prima time playing hide-and-seek among the trees and bushes."

"And you're both from Essex, is that right?" Bruce wondered.

"Yes, we're both from Cartford, Essex," said Octavia. "Next-door neighbours. We've been friends since first school."

"Didn't you ever fall out?" queried Duncan.

"Not really. We both became Christians when we were quite young, and probably the Holy Spirit helped us not to get too stroppy with each other," said Celia. "I believe that's what happened in my case, at least."

"Probably in my case, too," Octavia said, casting her

mind back to her childhood. She was unable to recall any serious quarrel.

As Duncan was contemplating the few light, fluffy clouds in the blue sky, he was reminded of something that not only the British Government, but also some of the other governments in the world had begun to do.

"I'm glad our government and some others are now getting rid of the most dangerous plutonium waste by shooting it away in rockets into the sun," he said. "I suppose it will be all right for the low-level radioactive waste to be buried deep underground in concrete containers."

"Yes, at least it's better than just leaving it and trying to forget about it!" commented Bruce. "But there's still one nuclear reactor left, that they haven't closed down yet. It's about time they did!"

The others agreed.

The conversation then turned to the subjects they were studying. Each thought the others' subjects must be really interesting, as well as their own chosen fields of study.

"Well, it would be a bit of a full file to try doing them all at once," Octavia observed.

"Speak for yourself!" teased her old friend. "How d'you know one of us isn't a genius!"

"You may've got something there," Bruce responded. "Our friend Duncan, here, although he's doing archaeology, is brilliant at maths, got excellent grades in the three sciences at school, and is a very good linguist!"

The girls were somewhat lost for words to learn that they did, indeed, appear to have a genius in their midst, and could only murmur expressions of wonder and admiration.

They reached the Glencoe area at about half past one, and the sun was still shining.

"I'll ignore the most spectacular mountains for today," Duncan announced, as he pulled over onto a flat place at the foot of some rocky ground which rose only gradually, as far as they could see.

"We're really lucky with the weather!" said Bruce with satisfaction, as he got out of the car and stretched out his arms. "I suppose we take the rucksacks now?"

Duncan confirmed that this was the plan, so the two young men struggled into the harnesses of the bulky-looking backpacks, while the girls picked up their smaller bags and remaining food supplies.

Duncan led the way, and at first the other three were able to walk side by side, but as the ground rose higher, Octavia held back to allow the other two to be ahead of her. Duncan looked round every now and then to check their progress, and Bruce was not far behind him.

Now the path was wide enough only for single file, so it was Bruce's turn to glance round every so often to see where the girls were.

Celia was not far behind, and Octavia was only a couple of metres behind her. The slope was not very steep, but here and there it was necessary to step over rocks which jutted out, or scramble up areas which seemed to consist of gravel.

They were now going in a kind of semicircular path, which involved mounting slabs of rock somewhat reminiscent of steps, and Duncan was no longer visible to Celia or Octavia.

Bruce came to a slab which was thicker and therefore higher than hitherto, and as he pulled himself up, he grabbed a spur of rock to aid his ascent. As he did so, there was a cracking noise, and his left foot came down with his full weight plus backpack onto Celia's left thumb, as she was clambering up behind.

"Aa-oh-oh-oo-oo . . .!" Her howl of agony resounded around the mountain slopes, and she slithered down in a faint, coming to rest just above Octavia.

"Oh no!" Bruce groaned, as he realised what had happened. "Duncan!" he shouted. "Come back here! Mayday! Mayday!"

Having seen her friend slipping down over the slabs of rock, Octavia thought Celia might have bumped her head a little in the process, but not too much. She lifted the girl's head carefully, but couldn't see any wound there, so she put her food pack under her head as a pillow. Then she looked at her friend's left thumb. It was covered in blood, and seemed to have been reduced to a pulp.

Bruce joined Octavia in staring at the mess which had been Celia's thumb, and a moment later Duncan climbed down to find out what was going on. He immediately shrugged his rucksack free, set it down, and located his first aid kit which was fitted into a pocket inside.

He produced a neatly packaged bandage. "This should help," he said, "but we need something to stop the bleeding. Has anyone got any tissues?"

Yes, Octavia had a pack in her bag, so Duncan very carefully put some crumpled tissues over the squashed thumb, then Bruce held them there, endeavouring not to press on the thumb in any way, whilst Duncan wound the bandage loosely around them.

"There now," he said, heaving a sigh of satisfaction that the job was completed, "I think that will do for the moment."

Then, when he was told what had happened, he continued thoughtfully, "I suppose a thumb isn't very serious, but she'll be suffering from shock. I don't know if your mobile phone will work here among the mountains, Octavia, but you can try dialling 999 for an ambulance while Bruce and I take it in turns to carry Celia down to the car. If she comes round in the meantime, we've got a flask of tea that should help."

*　*　*　*　*　*　*

Edith was enjoying catching up on her reading. It was Saturday afternoon, and she was comfortably ensconced in an armchair in the small lounge of her safe house, reading . . . Suddenly she emitted an intense howl of agony:

"Aa-oh-oh-oo-oo . . . !" The sound echoed through the house, as Edith lost consciousness through the pain.

Mike, the guard, came running to her door. Not receiving any reply, he peered in cautiously, and saw Edith slumped, unconscious, in the armchair.

He looked around the room sharply, but there was

no sign of any intruder. As he came closer, he was unable to see anything, such as a wound, that could have caused the terrible cry of pain.

Sam appeared in the doorway, followed soon afterwards by Cheryl.

"What's happened?" Sam asked, voicing his concern. "What was that terrible howl?"

He came further into the room, and saw Edith half lying in the armchair.

"I think she's fainted," Mike replied.

"I'll get her something to drink," said Cheryl, going into Edith's kitchen. She came back with a glass of water, and held it to the unconscious woman's lips.

Gradually Edith came to herself. "Ooooh! My thumb! It felt as if someone had hit it with a sledgehammer!" she said weakly. "It still feels like it!"

She was looking at her left thumb, and the other occupants of the room who had rushed to her rescue stared at the thumb, mystified. Then they looked at each other in bewilderment.

It was Cheryl who finally expressed what they were thinking. "I'm sorry dear," she said gently, "I can't see anything wrong with your thumb."

18

Celia regained consciousness after Duncan and Bruce had carried her down the mountain slopes for about fifteen minutes. Bruce rummaged in his backpack to find the flask, and Celia, who was now shaking, was given a welcome cup of tea. It revived her rapidly, so that she was able to walk to the car.

"I think we'd better get her to a hospital," said Duncan. He had been right in guessing that Octavia's mobile phone would be no use among these mountains.

"Before we do anything else, let's do a bit of praying," Duncan continued. He then led them in a prayer asking God to heal the thumb sufficiently for the medical staff at the nearest hospital to be able to deal with it in the most effective way.

Having enquired at a house in Altnafeadh, they learned that there was a hospital at Kinlochleven. "So that's where we'll go," Duncan said levelly. "The fuel cell is still half charged."

It was dark by the time they reached the hospital, but the first aid bandage on Celia's thumb had helped to reduce the bleeding.

An X-ray revealed that the bones in the thumb were smashed into tiny fragments. But when Celia's friends showed their concern about this, they were told there was nothing to worry about; setting the fragments of bone was no problem, but she should stay in the hospital overnight to make sure of recovering from the effects of the shock that Duncan had rightly anticipated.

The three friends decided to spend the night at a youth hostel just outside the town, so they promised to collect Celia for the drive back to St Andrew's at about nine o'clock next morning.

Celia now decided to telephone her parents, to let them know what had occurred. There was no reply except for the answermachine. But rather than leave a message on that, she dialled Paul Kellard's number.

He was full of concern when he heard about the mishap. "It must be horribly painful!" he commiserated. "Are you due to fly back on Monday?"

She confirmed that the return flight was booked for Monday, at which he said in his rich, vibrant voice, "If you like, I'll drive up to St Andrew's tomorrow, and bring you back with me on Monday. What d'you think?"

"Well, that's very kind of you to offer, but I should be all right to fly back, thank you."

"But don't forget you have to get a train from St Andrew's to Edinburgh. I think it would be much easier for you to come in the car."

"Mm-m I was forgetting about the train," Celia admitted. "Well, if you insist, I'd be very happy to come back with you. Thank you very much."

"Prima!" Paul exclaimed exultantly. "Give me your phone number for where you're staying, and I'll call you from whatever hotel I can find in the vicinity, OK?"

Having told him the phone number, Celia added, "And don't forget to pass on the message to my parents, please!"

Celia put down the receiver, bathed in a warm glow of contentment, in spite of the painful throbbing of her thumb. Paul's voice affected her like the bow of a cello being drawn across strings running down her spine. She guessed that he surely must have commitments as a hospital chaplain on a Sunday, but it seemed that he cared enough for her, to have to go to the trouble of finding someone to take over for him in his absence.

*　*　*　*　*　*　*

In the meantime Edith had come to the conclusion that Celia must have had an accident involving her thumb. She had tried to explain the phenomenon to Cheryl, Sam and Mike, when they stood staring at her thumb in perplexity.

"It must be my niece's pain that I'm feeling," she contrived to say, in spite of the throbbing in her thumb. "We're very close, a bit like twins, and sometimes we feel each other's pain. Maybe she caught her thumb in a car door, or something."

Her hearers considered this to be very weird, but they tried to be sympathetic as they went out of the room, hoping she would soon be free of the pain.

It persisted, however, for several hours, and Edith was reminded of what Jonathan had said: "I hope *you* never have to experience anything like that kind of torture!" The pain in her thumb had been excruciating, and was still severe, but she supposed it would be even worse if the nail were actually being torn out ...

She began to feel sorry that she had been so unfeeling; so lacking in sympathy for what Jonathan had suffered, including the threat of having the rest of his fingernails pulled out. It occurred to her that there probably were not many people who could endure torture without giving in to their tormentors. She now felt ashamed of her cold rebuff and dismissal of Jonathan.

At about seven o'clock that evening Edith dialled the hospital chaplain's number. Paul explained that he was just in the process of arranging to go to Scotland, and related the story of Celia's accident.

Edith was close to tears as she told Paul Kellard about the pain she had experienced in her left thumb, and how she needed to speak to Jonathan. She was trying not to go into too much detail, but Paul gathered that there was a need for some sort of reconciliation between herself and the professor.

"I'll try to get a message to him. Shall I say you'd like to see him as soon as possible?"

"Oh, yes please! That would be very helpful. I've been trying to ignore the bits in the New Testament that say you have to forgive. There's something I have to forgive Jonathan for."

"Well, that's excellent news, if you're going to forgive him. I'm glad you've come to realise how important it is."

"I have indeed. Thanks for your help, and give my love to Celia."

Paul promised to do so, and brought the conversation to a close.

Edith realised, as she put down the receiver, that she was feeling better already. The pain in her thumb was now moderately bearable, and she felt as though a heavy weight had been lifted from her shoulders.

Paul's attempts to contact Professor Jonathan Rymer were unsuccessful. It was difficult even to have a message relayed to him, for he was not at the safe house, and no one was able or willing to tell him of the professor's whereabouts.

"Well, if you *are* able to contact him in any way," he finally said to the policeman answering his call, "would you please tell him that Edith Owen needs to see him about an urgent matter. Thanks very much."

As he was finishing his preparations for the journey to Edinburgh, Paul debated with himself whether to ring Edith with the news that her professor friend was unavailable. 'I can't tell her he's disappeared,' he thought. 'And even if I just say he's gone away, it might sound ominous. I think I'd better leave it as it is, and just hope the professor is safe.'

He sat down on the chair next to his compunicunit and spent a few minutes praying for Prof. Rymer's protection.

*   *   *   *   *   *   *

"I hope it wasn't too difficult for you to find people to take over for you while you're away," Celia remarked as she and Paul began the drive south.

"Oh no," he replied blithely, "I usually take Sunday services in one of the big churches in Cartford town centre, as well as in the hospital, but there are always plenty of colleagues or lay preachers who are quite happy to step in at a moment's notice."

Celia and Paul appreciated the drive through the Scottish countryside, especially south of Edinburgh and in the Borders region, where they agreed that the views were superb.

Further south the landscape was considerably less spectacular, so they passed the time sharing their thoughts on what further improvements needed to be carried out to make Britain an even better Christian country.

"I think there are still too many violent American films being shown on television, even though revival has been happening in some states," said Celia. "I think the Government ought to subsidise British Christian film-makers more, so that people could watch really good films."

"I couldn't agree more," responded Paul. "And there are still some cartoons being shown that unwise parents let their small children watch, in spite of the parenting classes."

"Yes. But at least the worst ones have been banned, like the worst videos."

"What d'you think about the latest efforts to persuade the big landowners to give away or sell their land?" Paul asked. "I think the Government is on the right track in setting up an independent agency to advise on all the use or preservation of the land, don't you?"

"I think something should be done so that the arable land is used wisely. Perhaps the really big landowners should be told if they haven't sold some of it — a certain stipulated percentage, such as seventy-five percent — by a certain time, then the Government will acquire it."

"I'm not sure about that. I agree that the land needs to be managed wisely," responded Paul, "although it's a complex issue. But I see no reason why the injustices of previous centuries should be allowed to continue."

They both considered the difficulties and possibilities of the problem for several minutes, then a new question occurred to Celia.

"How do you feel when you're counselling patients in hospital, as Chaplain?" she asked. "Do you try to suppress all human emotion, like the Vulcans in the old Star Trek films?"

"Oh no. Christians shouldn't try to *suppress* their emotions. They can control them, by the power of the Holy Spirit, but certainly not suppress them. If they are aware of an emotion that's inappropriate, such as an infatuation for a married person, they should face it squarely, and pray to relinquish it. It's often possible then, for a Christian man or woman to get rid of the infatuation by regarding the person as a brother or sister, if possible keeping him or her at a distance."

"I see. Yes, now I come to think of it, Jesus showed emotions quite a few times."

"Right. But he didn't let himself be controlled by them. He controlled *them*."

After a moment or two Paul continued, "Love is not just an emotion; it's an act of the will. God commands us to love Him — to align our will with His. And in doing so, we may sometimes love Him emotionally, as when we contemplate the Cross, or discover some new wonder of His creation. Similarly, love for a spouse is to be primarily an act of the will."

Celia considered these thoughts for a while, then she asked, "D'you know whether the Revival has spread to the Czech Republic yet? I know it's been spreading through the other European countries like France, Belgium, Germany and Switzerland."

"Yes, I've read that it is spreading there. But it needs to happen throughout the United States, too."

"Yes, I know it's been happening in *some* parts of America," said Celia. "I suppose it will cover the whole country eventually. The trouble is that a lot of the worst criminals move to the states where Revival has affected everybody and everything, and they tend to disrupt the good things that have been introduced. But with all those people praying, the criminals will have to give up in the end."

They lingered over their afternoon tea stop with pancakes, cherries and icecream, so that darkness was already falling as they returned to the car. As Celia was beginning to operate her seat belt, Paul put a restraining hand over hers, and leaned towards her. He gently turned her face in his direction.

"Will you marry me?" he asked softly.

Celia couldn't believe her ears. "Are you serious?"

"I'm very serious. Very serious indeed. I'm glad there's still enough light for me to see your eyes. They remind me of a song my uncle used to sing."

Celia marvelled at the clear tones, as Paul began to sing, with his superb tenor voice:

The pale moon was rising above the green
                                        mountain,
The sun was declining beneath the blue sea
When I strayed with my love to the pure crystal
                                        fountain
That stands in the beautiful vale of Tralee.

She was lovely, and fair as the rose of the
                                        summer,
Yet 'twas not her beauty alone that won me;
Oh, no! 'Twas the truth in her eyes ever
                                        dawning
That made me love Mary, the rose of Tralee.

As he finished singing, Paul encircled Celia with his arms and kissed her tenderly for several minutes — moments which for both of them were filled with unparalleled rapture.

Finally Paul said, "Your eyes are just like that — full of truth as well as beauty. And I love them." Then a thought recurred: "You haven't answered my question. Will you marry me?"

"Oh yes! Yes! I'd love to marry you!"

19

The days turned into weeks without any word from Jonathan, or even Paul Kellard. Edith had been endeavouring not to worry, but now it was becoming almost impossible. Her guardian policewoman, Emma, had been unable to find out anything, and Sam told her there was no information available.

She had waylaid Mike, by standing at her door as he was on his way downstairs to collect his meals, but he was equally unable to help.

Edith's faith was too new and immature for her to be able to overcome anxiety, although she prayed every day for Jonathan's safety. The peace that she had begun to feel after deciding to forgive him had left her, replaced by restlessness and frustration.

At last she telephoned the hospital chaplain. Surely he could tell her something, she thought.

"No, I'm sorry, Edith," came his reply to her enquiry, "I'm afraid I wasn't able to speak to Jonathan when I tried. I was told he'd gone away. That's all they would tell me. But I did leave a message for him, saying that you needed to see him about an urgent matter."

"Really? Thanks. But I still haven't heard from him, and the police won't give me any information. I don't like the look of things." Her voice shook a little as she said these words, struggling to control herself.

"Well, I'm praying for his protection," said Paul, trying to sound comforting. "At least Celia's thumb is doing very well. It has healed amazingly quickly, and the nail is beginning to grow back already!"

Edith was reminded of the intense pain she had felt at the time in her own left thumb. She was also reminded, however, of the shame she had felt on reflecting how much Jonathan must have suffered under torture.

"Well, I'm glad her thumb is so much better now. Please try again sometime to see if you can discover anything about where Jonathan has disappeared to."

"OK, I'll give it another try. But just remember the incident when Jesus and his disciples were in a boat during a storm on Lake Galilee. Jesus was *asleep*, in spite of the waves coming over the side and the howling gale — there's faith for you! You can read it in

Mark's gospel. Chapter Four, I think."

"Yes, I will read it, if you think it'll help me to have more faith," Edith promised.

"By the way, did you know Celia and I will be getting married in the spring?"

"*What?!* Really?" she exclaimed excitedly. "No, I didn't know . . . Well, congratulations!" Edith was surprised to feel a tear rolling down her cheek, then she said, "You know Celia is really like my daughter, so that means you'll almost be my son-in-law! But I'm afraid I'll have to continue playing the role of auntie."

"Well, perhaps you can become Celia's favourite aunt in future, instead of the one she thought was spooky, and the one she sometimes hated!"

* * * * * * *

Edith felt as if she had been through a maelstrom. She was endeavouring to cope with joyful feelings about Paul and Celia's engagement, whilst at the same time trying not to be anxious about Jonathan.

She read the New Testament passage Paul had recommended, and sat pondering the nature of faith. Paul Kellard seemed to have no doubt at all that God would protect someone if we asked Him to do so.

But what about Celia's thumb? Surely her adoptive parents had prayed for her safety . . . Or perhaps they hadn't known she was going to Glencoe, and would need extra protection? It seemed to Edith that God had deliberately allowed the accident to happen, in order to teach her to forgive. 'But Celia didn't *have* to go to Glencoe,' she thought. 'And that student didn't *have* to fall back onto her thumb. . . God would have had to *intervene* to prevent it.'

A picture of the Israelites crossing the Red Sea on dry land came into her mind, followed by another of the Egyptians chasing them in their chariots, and the water returning to its normal flow, covering them and drowning them.

'He intervened only while the Israelites were crossing. After that He let nature take its course,' she said to herself.

Having reached that conclusion, Edith felt that perhaps she now had a little more faith to believe that God would grant her prayer for Jonathan's protection.

When Sam arrived at her door with her lunch, she invited him to stay for a moment to explain how he operated in the realm of faith.

"I see it as quite straightforward," he declared jovially. "God is like a perfect father, so He will grant

His children's requests if they're not contrary to His will. It's like a boy who has been promised a DVD writer by his father for Christmas. Even though it's a few weeks before Christmas, as far as the boy is concerned, he already *has* the DVD writer!"

Edith was halfway through praying with this kind of faith, when there was a knock at the door. It was Professor Jonathan Rymer.

"I understand you wanted to see me urgently," he said nonchalantly as he entered the room.

20

Edith attempted to retain her composure as she watched Jonathan come sauntering into the room.

"Please sit down," she said, somewhat dazed to find that her prayer had so obviously been granted. "Would you like a cup of tea or coffee?"

"I'd appreciate a cup of coffee, thanks."

She waited until they both had their coffee, then she said, with a great effort of self-control, "I'm sorry, Jonathan. I really am. I've been wanting to apologise for weeks. It was very unfeeling of me to react the way I did. I realise now there are not many heroes who can hold out under torture. I don't think *I* would be able to. Will you forgive me for the way I spoke to you?"

Jonathan had begun to drink his coffee, but as Edith's words became a plea for his forgiveness, he put down his cup and stared at her in astonishment.

"Of course I will. But what brought about this change of heart?"

Edith told him about the accident involving Celia's

thumb. "So I can't help thinking that God allowed it to happen, to teach me a lesson. It was double agony for me, because she's like my daughter really," she finished.

"Well," Jonathan said thoughtfully, "it could have been just coincidence. But all's well that ends well." He gave an enigmatic grin, and continued, "They left it to me to tell you the good news."

Now it was Edith's turn to show surprise. "What good news?" she enquired, mystified.

"We're free to leave our safe houses and go home!" he announced.

"Oh! Have they caught those jailbirds?"

"No. There had been a kind of revival in the prison where they'd been held, and all the newly-converted Christians had been praying for the same thing to happen to Ortiz and Rodriguez. I was on my way back from Ireland yesterday when I heard the news. They've become Christians and have given themselves up. They've agreed to serve the remainder of their sentences!"

Edith was so overjoyed that she flew over to Jonathan, who stood up to receive her embrace. They hugged each other for several minutes, until Jonathan spoke.

"I've got another piece of news that might interest

you. I've committed myself unreservedly to Jesus! I thought of myself as a Christian before, but I had quite a few reservations."

"Oh, that's wonderful!" Edith breathed, stepping back a little as Jonathan released her. She sat down in the other armchair, for his smile was different from before, and having its impact on her. She had always considered him to have a good-looking face, but his new smile seemed to combine the spiritual and physical in a way that illuminated all his features, confirming to Edith what she had long been trying to deny: he was the most attractive man she had ever met.

"How did it come about?" she asked.

"It was while I was visiting my mother in Ireland. She likes to have a nap in the afternoon, so I was left to my own devices. She uses a booklet called 'Every Day with Jesus', so I picked it up and had a look at it. The theme was the meaning of the cross. It was so interesting and well written that I read the whole thing.

"Thinking about him hanging on the cross, it occurred to me that, even if he hadn't had the pain of the nails through his wrists, and the unimaginable spiritual agony, the mere fact of not being able to brush away the blood that was probably still trickling down his face from the scratches caused by the crown of thorns, or the flies that would have been crawling over his face would have been torture in itself."

"Plus the humiliation of being stripped naked, especially after being highly respected by most people as a teacher and miracle-worker," Edith added.

"Then when I looked up the references to Isaiah 53 and some of the things Jesus had said, predicting his death, it all made sense, like the example given in the booklet. When a certain father saw his son killing himself with heroin, it wasn't enough to say, 'I forgive you'; some sort of action was needed. So he fasted almost to the point of death, and the son stopped his drug-taking in response. So, now I'm a new creation!"

"You probably feel like celebrating!" Edith suggested.

"You're right! Why don't we tell Sam and Cheryl downstairs. Maybe they'll join us in a celebration!"

Their two friends below stairs were delighted to entertain them for dinner down in the kitchen, and Sam even found some champagne for an extra little sparkle.

"Here's celebrating your spiritual birthday!" he declared, holding up his glass.

"May you grow into the likeness of Christ!" said Cheryl, as they all joined in the toast.

As they were enjoying the meal, Edith said, "I've just remembered another cause for celebration."

Looking in Jonathan's direction, she announced, "Celia and Paul Kellard are getting married in the spring!"

As the professor was recovering from the surprise, and staring at her enigmatically, Edith explained to their hosts who it was that she was referring to.

"Well, I hope she continues her studies," said Jonathan doubtfully.

"Oh, I'm sure she will. She doesn't give up easily, and I know she's fascinated by the subjects she's chosen."

Edith accepted Jonathan's offer to drive her home as soon as she could collect her belongings together after the meal.

"I think I can find room in the car for everything," he said hopefully, "even all your books! I've already taken my things home."

With not much spare space left when they had finished, they did succeed in stowing Edith's cases, bags and books in the MG, and bade a fond farewell to the occupants of the safe house.

As they drew near to Bishops Stortford, Jonathan remarked, "Your house will be very cold, after being left empty so long, even if Emma did leave a bit of heating on. It would be nicer for you to go home tomorrow morning, wouldn't it, so that it can warm up through the day."

"Mm-m, you're probably right," Edith replied, thinking it over.

"I know a very pleasant hotel in Sawbridgeworth," said Jonathan. "We could stay there for the night." Then he added, with a smile and a sideways glance at her, "In separate rooms, of course."

"Of course," Edith smiled. "Yes, that sounds like a nice idea. You must be quite tired, after your travels, and then a lot of driving today."

It was not until next morning after breakfast that Jonathan walked into Edith's room, took her in his arms and gave her a long, lingering kiss.

"I don't think a double wedding would be a good idea, under the circumstances," he said gently, stroking her hair. "People would wonder why they were seeing double! But if Celia and Paul are getting married in the spring, shall we aim at New Year's Day? Will you be my New Year bride? I think you'll agree we've been apart too long?"

"You're right, I do agree," Edith replied.

THE ESSENTIAL BOOK OF RECIPES FOR GOOD LIVING

EILEEN MOHR

A collection of 70 sermons (mostly quite short) with at least one for each letter of the alphabet. The author, who was a lay preacher, deals with a wide range of topics, including parenting, marriage, Alzheimer's disease, health and peace, giving valuable fresh insights into questions of modern life, with wise counsel for solving or avoiding life's problems.

Alec Motyer, writing in the European Christian Bookstore Journal, says: "I could find for you something quotable on every page; I would prefer you to find it for yourself."

Published with a choice of 4 different covers:
A: 'Bread and Wine' B: 'The Creation' C: 'A Woodland Path' D: Abstract based on an abbey.

ISBN 0 9524604 4 0 Paperback £5.99

Available from **Mohr Books**, 345 Old Birmingham Road, Bromsgrove, B60 1NX.

Also published by *Mohr Books*:

A WELL BROUGHT UP EASTENDER
E.H. (ERNIE) RELF

The fascinating true story of a boy who grew up in the East End of London in the early part of the last century, who was almost miraculously shielded from the brutality and coarse depravity that was so common all around him. Ernie tells how he is raised with a tendency to view almost everyone as being like his own family: good natured and well meaning.

Having proved his masculinity by developing his skill at boxing, one of his strong ambitions is to find a well-educated, well-bred wife. The consequences are tragically cruel. Ernie learns the hard way that life can have a darker side. This unusual Eastender shows remarkable resilience, however, and eventually finds happiness, not in London, but in Cornwall.

The reader wonders: was he *too* well raised?

Students of history, psychology and anthropology will find this book to be a mine of background information, with scenes of everyday life and descriptions of locations no longer existent in the East End of London.

ISBN 0 9524604 1 6 Hardback. Only £7.99 from *Mohr Books*, 345 Old Birmingham Road, Bromsgrove, B60 1NX

THUMBELINA

RUTH MARIA TAPP

Story for children with 18 delightful piano pieces to play and beautiful pictures to colour. Written to be performed (as well as to be played) by children using simple ballet-style dances, the suite gives many opportunities for teachers in schools to undertake activities which will fulfil the requirements of the National Curriculum Attainment Targets in Physical Education (Dance) and English (Speaking and Listening).

The story itself diverges considerably from the traditional tale, and the piano pieces cover a wide variety of ability, not arranged in order of difficulty. The teacher will be able to select which pieces to tackle first, and will appreciate the melodies provided, ensuring that the child will enjoy playing them and be encouraged to try some of the more difficult pieces.

A welcome opportunity for parents and teachers to supplement their children's repertoire.

18 piano pieces   Size: A4 £6.99   18 line drawings
ISBN 0 9524604 5 9   Available from:
345, Old Birmingham Road, Bromsgrove, B60 1NX.

Order Form

CROSSBRIDGE BOOKS

(incorporating *Mohr Books*)

345 Old Birmingham Road, Bromsgrove, B60 1NX, UK

Tel: 0121 447 7897 Fax: 0121 445 1063
e-mail: Mohr_Books@compuserve.com
www.mohrbooks.co.uk

To order books, return this order form to the address above, enclosing
your cheque or crossed postal order. Postage & packing is FREE..

Please send me the following books:

	R.R. Price	Special price	Qty.	Total
Mother Twin	~~£12.99~~	£10.00		£
It's True! (Hardback)	~~£10.99~~	£6.99		£
It's True! (Paperback)	£4.99	£4.99		£
Total Healing	£5.00	£5.00		£
The Kentle-Shaddy	£3.99	£3.99		£
Thumbelina	£6.99	£6.99		£
A Well Brought Up Eastender	~~£12.99~~	£7.99		£
The Essential Book of Recipes for Good Living Cover* A B C D	£5.99	£5.99		£
* Circle selected cover		Postage & packing		FREE
			Total	£

I enclose a cheque / postal order
(payable to CROSSBRIDGE BOOKS) for £ _____

Name:

Address:

Postcode:

This order form may be photocopied.